THE STOLEN BACILLUS
AND OTHER INCIDENTS

THE STOLEN BACILLUS AND OTHER INCIDENTS

HERBERT GEORGE WELLS

ISBN: 978-93-5342-920-1

First Published: 1895

LECTOR HOUSE LLP
E-MAIL: lectorpublishing@gmail.com

THE STOLEN BACILLUS AND OTHER INCIDENTS

BY

H.G. WELLS

AUTHOR OF "THE TIME MACHINE"

1895

TO
H.B. MARRIOTT WATSON

Most of the stories in this collection appeared originally in the *Pall Mall Budget*, two were published in the *Pall Mall Gazette*, and one in *St James's Gazette*. I desire to make the usual acknowledgments. The third story in the book was, I find, reprinted by the *Observatory*, and the "Lord of the Dynamos" by the Melbourne *Leader*.

H.G. WELLS.

CONTENTS

THE STOLEN BACILLUS

"This again," said the Bacteriologist, slipping a glass slide under the microscope, "is a preparation of the celebrated Bacillus of cholera—the cholera germ."

The pale-faced man peered down the microscope. He was evidently not accustomed to that kind of thing, and held a limp white hand over his disengaged eye. "I see very little," he said.

"Touch this screw," said the Bacteriologist; "perhaps the microscope is out of focus for you. Eyes vary so much. Just the fraction of a turn this way or that."

"Ah! now I see," said the visitor. "Not so very much to see after all. Little streaks and shreds of pink. And yet those little particles, those mere atomies, might multiply and devastate a city! Wonderful!"

He stood up, and releasing the glass slip from the microscope, held it in his hand towards the window. "Scarcely visible," he said, scrutinising the preparation. He hesitated. "Are these—alive? Are they dangerous now?"

"Those have been stained and killed," said the Bacteriologist. "I wish, for my own part, we could kill and stain every one of them in the universe."

"I suppose," the pale man said with a slight smile, "that you scarcely care to have such things about you in the living—in the active state?"

"On the contrary, we are obliged to," said the Bacteriologist. "Here, for instance—" He walked across the room and took up one of several sealed tubes. "Here is the living thing. This is a cultivation of the actual living disease bacteria." He hesitated, "Bottled cholera, so to speak."

A slight gleam of satisfaction appeared momentarily in the face of the pale man.

"It's a deadly thing to have in your possession," he said, devouring the little tube with his eyes. The Bacteriologist watched the morbid pleasure in his visitor's expression. This man, who had visited him that afternoon with a note of introduction from an old friend, interested him from the very contrast of their dispositions. The lank black hair and deep grey eyes, the haggard expression and nervous manner, the fitful yet keen interest of his visitor were a novel change from the phlegmatic deliberations of the ordinary scientific worker with whom the Bacteriologist chiefly associated. It was perhaps natural, with a hearer evidently so impressionable to the lethal nature of his topic, to take the most effective aspect of the matter.

He held the tube in his hand thoughtfully. "Yes, here is the pestilence imprisoned. Only break such a little tube as this into a supply of drinking-water, say to these minute particles of life that one must needs stain and examine with the highest powers of the microscope even to see, and that one can neither smell nor taste—say to them, 'Go forth, increase and multiply, and replenish the cisterns,' and death—mysterious, untraceable death, death swift and terrible, death full of pain and indignity—would be released upon this city, and go hither and thither seeking his victims. Here he would take the husband from the wife, here the child from its mother, here the statesman from his duty, and here the toiler from his trouble. He would follow the water-mains, creeping along streets, picking out and punishing a house here and a house there where they did not boil their drinking-water, creeping into the wells of the mineral-water makers, getting washed into salad, and lying dormant in ices. He would wait ready to be drunk in the horse-troughs, and by unwary children in the public fountains. He would soak into the soil, to reappear in springs and wells at a thousand unexpected places. Once start him at the water supply, and before we could ring him in, and catch him again, he would have decimated the metropolis."

He stopped abruptly. He had been told rhetoric was his weakness.

"But he is quite safe here, you know—quite safe."

The pale-faced man nodded. His eyes shone. He cleared his throat. "These Anarchist—rascals," said he, "are fools, blind fools—to use bombs when this kind of thing is attainable. I think—"

A gentle rap, a mere light touch of the finger-nails was heard at the door. The Bacteriologist opened it. "Just a minute, dear," whispered his wife.

When he re-entered the laboratory his visitor was looking at his watch. "I had no idea I had wasted an hour of your time," he said. "Twelve minutes to four. I ought to have left here by half-past three. But your things were really too interesting. No, positively I cannot stop a moment longer. I have an engagement at four."

He passed out of the room reiterating his thanks, and the Bacteriologist accompanied him to the door, and then returned thoughtfully along the passage to his laboratory. He was musing on the ethnology of his visitor. Certainly the man was not a Teutonic type nor a common Latin one. "A morbid product, anyhow, I am afraid," said the Bacteriologist to himself. "How he gloated on those cultivations of disease-germs!" A disturbing thought struck him. He turned to the bench by the vapour-bath, and then very quickly to his writing-table. Then he felt hastily in his pockets, and then rushed to the door. "I may have put it down on the hall table," he said.

"Minnie!" he shouted hoarsely in the hall.

"Yes, dear," came a remote voice.

"Had I anything in my hand when I spoke to you, dear, just now?"

Pause.

"Nothing, dear, because I remember—"

"Blue ruin!" cried the Bacteriologist, and incontinently ran to the front door and down the steps of his house to the street.

Minnie, hearing the door slam violently, ran in alarm to the window. Down the street a slender man was getting into a cab. The Bacteriologist, hatless, and in his carpet slippers, was running and gesticulating wildly towards this group. One slipper came off, but he did not wait for it. "He has gone *mad!*" said Minnie; "it's that horrid science of his"; and, opening the window, would have called after him. The slender man, suddenly glancing round, seemed struck with the same idea of mental disorder. He pointed hastily to the Bacteriologist, said something to the cabman, the apron of the cab slammed, the whip swished, the horse's feet clattered, and in a moment cab, and Bacteriologist hotly in pursuit, had receded up the vista of the roadway and disappeared round the corner.

Minnie remained straining out of the window for a minute. Then she drew her head back into the room again. She was dumbfounded. "Of course he is eccentric," she meditated. "But running about London—in the height of the season, too—in his socks!" A happy thought struck her. She hastily put her bonnet on, seized his shoes, went into the hall, took down his hat and light overcoat from the pegs, emerged upon the doorstep, and hailed a cab that opportunely crawled by. "Drive me up the road and round Havelock Crescent, and see if we can find a gentleman running about in a velveteen coat and no hat."

"Velveteen coat, ma'am, and no 'at. Very good, ma'am." And the cabman whipped up at once in the most matter-of-fact way, as if he drove to this address every day in his life.

Some few minutes later the little group of cabmen and loafers that collects round the cabmen's shelter at Haverstock Hill were startled by the passing of a cab with a ginger-coloured screw of a horse, driven furiously.

They were silent as it went by, and then as it receded—"That's 'Arry 'Icks. Wot's *he* got?" said the stout gentleman known as Old Tootles.

"He's a-using his whip, he is, *to* rights," said the ostler boy.

"Hullo!" said poor old Tommy Byles; "here's another bloomin' loonatic. Blowed if there aint."

"It's old George," said old Tootles, "and he's drivin' a loonatic, *as* you say. Aint he a-clawin' out of the keb? Wonder if he's after 'Arry 'Icks?"

The group round the cabmen's shelter became animated. Chorus: "Go it, George!" "It's a race." "You'll ketch 'em!" "Whip up!"

"She's a goer, she is!" said the ostler boy.

"Strike me giddy!" cried old Tootles. "Here! *I'm* a-goin' to begin in a minute. Here's another comin'. If all the kebs in Hampstead aint gone mad this morning!"

"It's a fieldmale this time," said the ostler boy.

"She's a followin' *him*," said old Tootles. "Usually the other way about."

"What's she got in her 'and?"

"Looks like a 'igh 'at."

"What a bloomin' lark it is! Three to one on old George," said the ostler boy. "Nexst!"

Minnie went by in a perfect roar of applause. She did not like it but she felt that she was doing her duty, and whirled on down Haverstock Hill and Camden Town High Street with her eyes ever intent on the animated back view of old George, who was driving her vagrant husband so incomprehensibly away from her.

The man in the foremost cab sat crouched in the corner, his arms tightly folded, and the little tube that contained such vast possibilities of destruction gripped in his hand. His mood was a singular mixture of fear and exultation. Chiefly he was afraid of being caught before he could accomplish his purpose, but behind this was a vaguer but larger fear of the awfulness of his crime. But his exultation far exceeded his fear. No Anarchist before him had ever approached this conception of his. Ravachol, Vaillant, all those distinguished persons whose fame he had envied dwindled into insignificance beside him. He had only to make sure of the water supply, and break the little tube into a reservoir. How brilliantly he had planned it, forged the letter of introduction and got into the laboratory, and how brilliantly he had seized his opportunity! The world should hear of him at last. All those people who had sneered at him, neglected him, preferred other people to him, found his company undesirable, should consider him at last. Death, death, death! They had always treated him as a man of no importance. All the world had been in a conspiracy to keep him under. He would teach them yet what it is to isolate a man. What was this familiar street? Great Saint Andrew's Street, of course! How fared the chase? He craned out of the cab. The Bacteriologist was scarcely fifty yards behind. That was bad. He would be caught and stopped yet. He felt in his pocket for money, and found half-a-sovereign. This he thrust up through the trap in the top of the cab into the man's face. "More," he shouted, "if only we get away."

The money was snatched out of his hand. "Right you are," said the cabman, and the trap slammed, and the lash lay along the glistening side of the horse. The cab swayed, and the Anarchist, half-standing under the trap, put the hand containing the little glass tube upon the apron to preserve his balance. He felt the brittle thing crack, and the broken half of it rang upon the floor of the cab. He fell back into the seat with a curse, and stared dismally at the two or three drops of moisture on the apron.

He shuddered.

"Well! I suppose I shall be the first. *Phew*! Anyhow, I shall be a Martyr. That's something. But it is a filthy death, nevertheless. I wonder if it hurts as much as they say."

Presently a thought occurred to him—he groped between his feet. A little drop was still in the broken end of the tube, and he drank that to make sure. It was better to make sure. At any rate, he would not fail.

Then it dawned upon him that there was no further need to escape the Bacteriologist. In Wellington Street he told the cabman to stop, and got out. He slipped on the step, and his head felt queer. It was rapid stuff this cholera poison. He waved his cabman out of existence, so to speak, and stood on the pavement with his arms folded upon his breast awaiting the arrival of the Bacteriologist. There was something tragic in his pose. The sense of imminent death gave him a certain dignity. He greeted his pursuer with a defiant laugh.

"Vive l'Anarchie! You are too late, my friend. I have drunk it. The cholera is abroad!"

The Bacteriologist from his cab beamed curiously at him through his spectacles. "You have drunk it! An Anarchist! I see now." He was about to say something more, and then checked himself. A smile hung in the corner of his mouth. He opened the apron of his cab as if to descend, at which the Anarchist waved him a dramatic farewell and strode off towards Waterloo Bridge, carefully jostling his infected body against as many people as possible. The Bacteriologist was so preoccupied with the vision of him that he scarcely manifested the slightest surprise at the appearance of Minnie upon the pavement with his hat and shoes and overcoat. "Very good of you to bring my things," he said, and remained lost in contemplation of the receding figure of the Anarchist.

"You had better get in," he said, still staring. Minnie felt absolutely convinced now that he was mad, and directed the cabman home on her own responsibility. "Put on my shoes? Certainly dear," said he, as the cab began to turn, and hid the strutting black figure, now small in the distance, from his eyes. Then suddenly something grotesque struck him, and he laughed. Then he remarked, "It is really very serious, though."

"You see, that man came to my house to see me, and he is an Anarchist. No—don't faint, or I cannot possibly tell you the rest. And I wanted to astonish him, not knowing he was an Anarchist, and took up a cultivation of that new species of Bacterium I was telling you of, that infest, and I think cause, the blue patches upon various monkeys; and like a fool, I said it was Asiatic cholera. And he ran away with it to poison the water of London, and he certainly might have made things look blue for this civilised city. And now he has swallowed it. Of course, I cannot say what will happen, but you know it turned that kitten blue, and the three puppies—in patches, and the sparrow—bright blue. But the bother is, I shall have all the trouble and expense of preparing some more.

"Put on my coat on this hot day! Why? Because we might meet Mrs Jabber. My dear, Mrs Jabber is not a draught. But why should I wear a coat on a hot day because of Mrs—. Oh! *very* well."

THE FLOWERING OF THE STRANGE OR-CHID

The buying of orchids always has in it a certain speculative flavour. You have before you the brown shrivelled lump of tissue, and for the rest you must trust your judgment, or the auctioneer, or your good-luck, as your taste may incline. The plant may be moribund or dead, or it may be just a respectable purchase, fair value for your money, or perhaps—for the thing has happened again and again— there slowly unfolds before the delighted eyes of the happy purchaser, day after day, some new variety, some novel richness, a strange twist of the labellum, or some subtler colouration or unexpected mimicry. Pride, beauty, and profit blossom together on one delicate green spike, and, it may be, even immortality. For the new miracle of Nature may stand in need of a new specific name, and what so convenient as that of its discoverer? "Johnsmithia"! There have been worse names.

It was perhaps the hope of some such happy discovery that made Winter-Wedderburn such a frequent attendant at these sales—that hope, and also, maybe, the fact that he had nothing else of the slightest interest to do in the world. He was a shy, lonely, rather ineffectual man, provided with just enough income to keep off the spur of necessity, and not enough nervous energy to make him seek any exacting employments. He might have collected stamps or coins, or translated Horace, or bound books, or invented new species of diatoms. But, as it happened, he grew orchids, and had one ambitious little hothouse.

"I have a fancy," he said over his coffee, "that something is going to happen to me to-day." He spoke—as he moved and thought—slowly.

"Oh, don't say *that!*" said his housekeeper—who was also his remote cousin. For "something happening" was a euphemism that meant only one thing to her.

"You misunderstand me. I mean nothing unpleasant ... though what I do mean I scarcely know.

"To-day," he continued, after a pause, "Peters' are going to sell a batch of plants from the Andamans and the Indies. I shall go up and see what they have. It may be I shall buy something good, unawares. That may be it."

He passed his cup for his second cupful of coffee.

"Are these the things collected by that poor young fellow you told me of the other day?" asked his cousin as she filled his cup.

"Yes," he said, and became meditative over a piece of toast.

"Nothing ever does happen to me," he remarked presently, beginning to think aloud. "I wonder why? Things enough happen to other people. There is Harvey. Only the other week; on Monday he picked up sixpence, on Wednesday his chicks all had the staggers, on Friday his cousin came home from Australia, and on Saturday he broke his ankle. What a whirl of excitement!—compared to me."

"I think I would rather be without so much excitement," said his housekeeper. "It can't be good for you."

"I suppose it's troublesome. Still … you see, nothing ever happens to me. When I was a little boy I never had accidents. I never fell in love as I grew up. Never married…. I wonder how it feels to have something happen to you, something really remarkable.

"That orchid-collector was only thirty-six—twenty years younger than myself—when he died. And he had been married twice and divorced once; he had had malarial fever four times, and once he broke his thigh. He killed a Malay once, and once he was wounded by a poisoned dart. And in the end he was killed by jungle-leeches. It must have all been very troublesome, but then it must have been very interesting, you know—except, perhaps, the leeches."

"I am sure it was not good for him," said the lady, with conviction.

"Perhaps not." And then Wedderburn looked at his watch. "Twenty-three minutes past eight. I am going up by the quarter to twelve train, so that there is plenty of time. I think I shall wear my alpaca jacket—it is quite warm enough—and my grey felt hat and brown shoes. I suppose—"

He glanced out of the window at the serene sky and sunlit garden, and then nervously at his cousin's face.

"I think you had better take an umbrella if you are going to London," she said in a voice that admitted of no denial. "There's all between here and the station coming back."

When he returned he was in a state of mild excitement. He had made a purchase. It was rare that he could make up his mind quickly enough to buy, but this time he had done so.

"There are Vandas," he said, "and a Dendrobe and some Palaeonophis." He surveyed his purchases lovingly as he consumed his soup. They were laid out on the spotless tablecloth before him, and he was telling his cousin all about them as he slowly meandered through his dinner. It was his custom to live all his visits to London over again in the evening for her and his own entertainment.

"I knew something would happen to-day. And I have bought all these. Some of them—some of them—I feel sure, do you know, that some of them will be remarkable. I don't know how it is, but I feel just as sure as if someone had told me that some of these will turn out remarkable."

"That one"—he pointed to a shrivelled rhizome—"was not identified. It may be a Palaeonophis—or it may not. It may be a new species, or even a new genus. And it was the last that poor Batten ever collected."

"I don't like the look of it," said his housekeeper. "It's such an ugly shape."

"To me it scarcely seems to have a shape."

"I don't like those things that stick out," said his housekeeper.

"It shall be put away in a pot to-morrow."

"It looks," said the housekeeper, "like a spider shamming dead."

Wedderburn smiled and surveyed the root with his head on one side. "It is certainly not a pretty lump of stuff. But you can never judge of these things from their dry appearance. It may turn out to be a very beautiful orchid indeed. How busy I shall be to-morrow! I must see to-night just exactly what to do with these things, and to-morrow I shall set to work."

"They found poor Batten lying dead, or dying, in a mangrove swamp—I forget which," he began again presently, "with one of these very orchids crushed up under his body. He had been unwell for some days with some kind of native fever, and I suppose he fainted. These mangrove swamps are very unwholesome. Every drop of blood, they say, was taken out of him by the jungle-leeches. It may be that very plant that cost him his life to obtain."

"I think none the better of it for that."

"Men must work though women may weep," said Wedderburn with profound gravity.

"Fancy dying away from every comfort in a nasty swamp! Fancy being ill of fever with nothing to take but chlorodyne and quinine—if men were left to themselves they would live on chlorodyne and quinine—and no one round you but horrible natives! They say the Andaman islanders are most disgusting wretches—and, anyhow, they can scarcely make good nurses, not having the necessary training. And just for people in England to have orchids!"

"I don't suppose it was comfortable, but some men seem to enjoy that kind of thing," said Wedderburn. "Anyhow, the natives of his party were sufficiently civilised to take care of all his collection until his colleague, who was an ornithologist, came back again from the interior; though they could not tell the species of the orchid and had let it wither. And it makes these things more interesting."

"It makes them disgusting. I should be afraid of some of the malaria clinging to them. And just think, there has been a dead body lying across that ugly thing! I never thought of that before. There! I declare I cannot eat another mouthful of dinner."

"I will take them off the table if you like, and put them in the window-seat. I can see them just as well there."

The next few days he was indeed singularly busy in his steamy little hothouse, fussing about with charcoal, lumps of teak, moss, and all the other mysteries of the orchid cultivator. He considered he was having a wonderfully eventful time. In the evening he would talk about these new orchids to his friends, and over and over again he reverted to his expectation of something strange.

Several of the Vandas and the Dendrobium died under his care, but presently the strange orchid began to show signs of life. He was delighted and took his housekeeper right away from jam-making to see it at once, directly he made the discovery.

"That is a bud," he said, "and presently there will be a lot of leaves there, and those little things coming out here are aërial rootlets."

"They look to me like little white fingers poking out of the brown," said his housekeeper. "I don't like them."

"Why not?"

"I don't know. They look like fingers trying to get at you. I can't help my likes and dislikes."

"I don't know for certain, but I don't *think* there are any orchids I know that have aërial rootlets quite like that. It may be my fancy, of course. You see they are a little flattened at the ends."

"I don't like 'em," said his housekeeper, suddenly shivering and turning away. "I know it's very silly of me—and I'm very sorry, particularly as you like the thing so much. But I can't help thinking of that corpse."

"But it may not be that particular plant. That was merely a guess of mine."

His housekeeper shrugged her shoulders. "Anyhow I don't like it," she said.

Wedderburn felt a little hurt at her dislike to the plant. But that did not prevent his talking to her about orchids generally, and this orchid in particular, whenever he felt inclined.

"There are such queer things about orchids," he said one day; "such possibilities of surprises. You know, Darwin studied their fertilisation, and showed that the whole structure of an ordinary orchid-flower was contrived in order that moths might carry the pollen from plant to plant. Well, it seems that there are lots of orchids known the flower of which cannot possibly be used for fertilisation in that way. Some of the Cypripediums, for instance; there are no insects known that can possibly fertilise them, and some of them have never be found with seed."

"But how do they form new plants?"

"By runners and tubers, and that kind of outgrowth. That is easily explained. The puzzle is, what are the flowers for?

"Very likely," he added, "*my* orchid may be something extraordinary in that way. If so I shall study it. I have often thought of making researches as Darwin did. But hitherto I have not found the time, or something else has happened to prevent it. The leaves are beginning to unfold now. I do wish you would come and see them!"

But she said that the orchid-house was so hot it gave her the headache. She had seen the plant once again, and the aërial rootlets, which were now some of them more than a foot long, had unfortunately reminded her of tentacles reaching out after something; and they got into her dreams, growing after her with incredible rapidity. So that she had settled to her entire satisfaction that she would not see that plant again, and Wedderburn had to admire its leaves alone. They were of the ordinary broad form, and a deep glossy green, with splashes and dots of deep red towards the base. He knew of no other leaves quite like them. The plant was placed on a low bench near the thermometer, and close by was a simple arrangement by which a tap dripped on the hot-water pipes and kept the air steamy. And he spent his afternoons now with some regularity meditating on the approaching flowering of this strange plant.

And at last the great thing happened. Directly he entered the little glass house he knew that the spike had burst out, although his great *Palaeonophis Lowii* hid the corner where his new darling stood. There was a new odour in the air, a rich, intensely sweet scent, that overpowered every other in that crowded, steaming little greenhouse.

Directly he noticed this he hurried down to the strange orchid. And, behold! the trailing green spikes bore now three great splashes of blossom, from which this overpowering sweetness proceeded. He stopped before them in an ecstasy of admiration.

The flowers were white, with streaks of golden orange upon the petals; the heavy labellum was coiled into an intricate projection, and a wonderful bluish purple mingled there with the gold. He could see at once that the genus was altogether a new one. And the insufferable scent! How hot the place was! The blossoms swam before his eyes.

He would see if the temperature was right. He made a step towards the thermometer. Suddenly everything appeared unsteady. The bricks on the floor were dancing up and down. Then the white blossoms, the green leaves behind them, the whole greenhouse, seemed to sweep sideways, and then in a curve upward.

* * * * *

At half-past four his cousin made the tea, according to their invariable custom. But Wedderburn did not come in for his tea.

"He is worshipping that horrid orchid," she told herself, and waited ten minutes. "His watch must have stopped. I will go and call him."

She went straight to the hothouse, and, opening the door, called his name. There was no reply. She noticed that the air was very close, and loaded with an intense perfume. Then she saw something lying on the bricks between the hot-water pipes.

For a minute, perhaps, she stood motionless.

He was lying, face upward, at the foot of the strange orchid. The tentacle-like aërial rootlets no longer swayed freely in the air, but were crowded together, a tangle of grey ropes, and stretched tight with their ends closely applied to his chin and neck and hands.

She did not understand. Then she saw from under one of the exultant tentacles upon his cheek there trickled a little thread of blood.

With an inarticulate cry she ran towards him, and tried to pull him away from the leech-like suckers. She snapped two of these tentacles, and their sap dripped red.

Then the overpowering scent of the blossom began to make her head reel. How they clung to him! She tore at the tough ropes, and he and the white inflorescence swam about her. She felt she was fainting, knew she must not. She left him and hastily opened the nearest door, and, after she had panted for a moment in the fresh air, she had a brilliant inspiration. She caught up a flower-pot and smashed in the windows at the end of the green-house. Then she re-entered. She tugged now with renewed strength at Wedderburn's motionless body, and brought the strange orchid crashing to the floor. It still clung with the grimmest tenacity to its victim. In a frenzy, she lugged it and him into the open air.

Then she thought of tearing through the sucker rootlets one by one, and in another minute she had released him and was dragging him away from the horror.

He was white and bleeding from a dozen circular patches.

The odd-job man was coming up the garden, amazed at the smashing of glass, and saw her emerge, hauling the inanimate body with red-stained hands. For a moment he thought impossible things.

"Bring some water!" she cried, and her voice dispelled his fancies. When, with unnatural alacrity, he returned with the water, he found her weeping with excitement, and with Wedderburn's head upon her knee, wiping the blood from his face.

"What's the matter?" said Wedderburn, opening his eyes feebly, and closing them again at once.

"Go and tell Annie to come out here to me, and then go for Doctor Haddon at once," she said to the odd-job man so soon as he brought the water; and added, seeing he hesitated, "I will tell you all about it when you come back."

Presently Wedderburn opened his eyes again, and, seeing that he was troubled by the puzzle of his position, she explained to him, "You fainted in the hothouse."

"And the orchid?"

"I will see to that," she said.

Wedderburn had lost a good deal of blood, but beyond that he had suffered no very great injury. They gave him brandy mixed with some pink extract of meat, and carried him upstairs to bed. His housekeeper told her incredible story in fragments to Dr Haddon. "Come to the orchid-house and see," she said.

The cold outer air was blowing in through the open door, and the sickly perfume was almost dispelled. Most of the torn aërial rootlets lay already withered amidst a number of dark stains upon the bricks. The stem of the inflorescence was broken by the fall of the plant, and the flowers were growing limp and brown at the edges of the petals. The doctor stooped towards it, then saw that one of the aërial rootlets still stirred feebly, and hesitated.

The next morning the strange orchid still lay there, black now and putrescent. The door banged intermittently in the morning breeze, and all the array of

Wedderburn's orchids was shrivelled and prostrate. But Wedderburn himself was bright and garrulous upstairs in the glory of his strange adventure.

IN THE AVU OBSERVATORY

The observatory at Avu, in Borneo, stands on the spur of the mountain. To the north rises the old crater, black at night against the unfathomable blue of the sky. From the little circular building, with its mushroom dome, the slopes plunge steeply downward into the black mysteries of the tropical forest beneath. The little house in which the observer and his assistant live is about fifty yards from the observatory, and beyond this are the huts of their native attendants.

Thaddy, the chief observer, was down with a slight fever. His assistant, Woodhouse, paused for a moment in silent contemplation of the tropical night before commencing his solitary vigil. The night was very still. Now and then voices and laughter came from the native huts, or the cry of some strange animal was heard from the midst of the mystery of the forest. Nocturnal insects appeared in ghostly fashion out of the darkness, and fluttered round his light. He thought, perhaps, of all the possibilities of discovery that still lay in the black tangle beneath him; for to the naturalist the virgin forests of Borneo are still a wonderland full of strange questions and half-suspected discoveries. Woodhouse carried a small lantern in his hand, and its yellow glow contrasted vividly with the infinite series of tints between lavender-blue and black in which the landscape was painted. His hands and face were smeared with ointment against the attacks of the mosquitoes.

Even in these days of celestial photography, work done in a purely temporary erection, and with only the most primitive appliances in addition to the telescope, still involves a very large amount of cramped and motionless watching. He sighed as he thought of the physical fatigues before him, stretched himself, and entered the observatory.

The reader is probably familiar with the structure of an ordinary astronomical observatory. The building is usually cylindrical in shape, with a very light hemispherical roof capable of being turned round from the interior. The telescope is supported upon a stone pillar in the centre, and a clockwork arrangement compensates for the earth's rotation, and allows a star once found to be continuously observed. Besides this, there is a compact tracery of wheels and screws about its point of support, by which the astronomer adjusts it. There is, of course, a slit in the movable roof which follows the eye of the telescope in its survey of the heavens. The observer sits or lies on a sloping wooden arrangement, which he can wheel to any part of the observatory as the position of the telescope may require. Within it is advisable to have things as dark as possible, in order to enhance the brilliance of the stars observed.

The lantern flared as Woodhouse entered his circular den, and the general darkness fled into black shadows behind the big machine, from which it presently seemed to creep back over the whole place again as the light waned. The slit was a profound transparent blue, in which six stars shone with tropical brilliance, and their light lay, a pallid gleam, along the black tube of the instrument. Woodhouse shifted the roof, and then proceeding to the telescope, turned first one wheel and then another, the great cylinder slowly swinging into a new position. Then he glanced through the finder, the little companion telescope, moved the roof a little more, made some further adjustments, and set the clockwork in motion. He took off his jacket, for the night was very hot, and pushed into position the uncomfortable seat to which he was condemned for the next four hours. Then with a sigh he resigned himself to his watch upon the mysteries of space.

There was no sound now in the observatory, and the lantern waned steadily. Outside there was the occasional cry of some animal in alarm or pain, or calling to its mate, and the intermittent sounds of the Malay and Dyak servants. Presently one of the men began a queer chanting song, in which the others joined at intervals. After this it would seem that they turned in for the night, for no further sound came from their direction, and the whispering stillness became more and more profound.

The clockwork ticked steadily. The shrill hum of a mosquito explored the place and grew shriller in indignation at Woodhouse's ointment. Then the lantern went out and all the observatory was black.

Woodhouse shifted his position presently, when the slow movement of the telescope had carried it beyond the limits of his comfort.

He was watching a little group of stars in the Milky Way, in one of which his chief had seen or fancied a remarkable colour variability. It was not a part of the regular work for which the establishment existed, and for that reason perhaps Woodhouse was deeply interested. He must have forgotten things terrestrial. All his attention was concentrated upon the great blue circle of the telescope field—a circle powdered, so it seemed, with an innumerable multitude of stars, and all luminous against the blackness of its setting. As he watched he seemed to himself to become incorporeal, as if he too were floating in the ether of space. Infinitely remote was the faint red spot he was observing.

Suddenly the stars were blotted out. A flash of blackness passed, and they were visible again.

"Queer," said Woodhouse. "Must have been a bird."

The thing happened again, and immediately after the great tube shivered as though it had been struck. Then the dome of the observatory resounded with a series of thundering blows. The stars seemed to sweep aside as the telescope—which had been undamped—swung round and away from the slit in the roof.

"Great Scott!" cried Woodhouse. "What's this?"

Some huge vague black shape, with a flapping something like a wing, seemed to be struggling in the aperture of the roof. In another moment the slit was clear again, and the luminous haze of the Milky Way shone warm and bright.

The interior of the roof was perfectly black, and only a scraping sound marked the whereabouts of the unknown creature.

Woodhouse had scrambled from the seat to his feet. He was trembling violently and in a perspiration with the suddenness of the occurrence. Was the thing, whatever it was, inside or out? It was big, whatever else it might be. Something shot across the skylight, and the telescope swayed. He started violently and put his arm up. It was in the observatory, then, with him. It was clinging to the roof, apparently. What the devil was it? Could it see him?

He stood for perhaps a minute in a state of stupefaction. The beast, whatever it was, clawed at the interior of the dome, and then something flapped almost into his face, and he saw the momentary gleam of starlight on a skin like oiled leather. His water-bottle was knocked off his little table with a smash.

The sense of some strange bird-creature hovering a few yards from his face in the darkness was indescribably unpleasant to Woodhouse. As his thought returned he concluded that it must be some night-bird or large bat. At any risk he would see what it was, and pulling a match from his pocket, he tried to strike it on the telescope seat. There was a smoking streak of phosphorescent light, the match flared for a moment, and he saw a vast wing sweeping towards him, a gleam of grey-brown fur, and then he was struck in the face and the match knocked out of his hand. The blow was aimed at his temple, and a claw tore sideways down to his cheek. He reeled and fell, and he heard the extinguished lantern smash. Another blow followed as he fell. He was partly stunned, he felt his own warm blood stream out upon his face. Instinctively he felt his eyes had been struck at, and, turning over on his face to protect them, tried to crawl under the protection of the telescope. He was struck again upon the back, and he heard his jacket rip, and then the thing hit the roof of the observatory. He edged as far as he could between the wooden seat and the eyepiece of the instrument, and turned his body round so that it was chiefly his feet that were exposed. With these he could at least kick. He was still in a mystified state. The strange beast banged about in the darkness, and presently clung to the telescope, making it sway and the gear rattle. Once it flapped near him, and he kicked out madly and felt a soft body with his feet. He was horribly scared now. It must be a big thing to swing the telescope like that. He saw for a moment the outline of a head black against the starlight, with sharply-pointed upstanding ears and a crest between them. It seemed to him to be as big as a mastiff's. Then he began to bawl out as loudly as he could for help.

At that the thing came down upon him again. As it did so his hand touched something beside him on the floor. He kicked out, and the next moment his ankle was gripped and held by a row of keen teeth. He yelled again, and tried to free his leg by kicking with the other. Then he realised he had the broken water-bottle at his hand, and, snatching it, he struggled into a sitting posture, and feeling in the darkness towards his foot, gripped a velvety ear, like the ear of a big cat. He had seized the water-bottle by its neck and brought it down with a shivering crash upon the head of the strange beast. He repeated the blow, and then stabbed and jobbed with the jagged end of it, in the darkness, where he judged the face might be.

The small teeth relaxed their hold, and at once Woodhouse pulled his leg free and kicked hard. He felt the sickening feel of fur and bone giving under his boot. There was a tearing bite at his arm, and he struck over it at the face, as he judged, and hit damp fur.

There was a pause; then he heard the sound of claws and the dragging of a heavy body away from him over the observatory floor. Then there was silence, broken only by his own sobbing breathing, and a sound like licking. Everything was black except the parallelogram of the blue skylight with the luminous dust of stars, against which the end of the telescope now appeared in silhouette. He waited, as it seemed, an interminable time. Was the thing coming on again? He felt in his trouser-pocket for some matches, and found one remaining. He tried to strike this, but the floor was wet, and it spat and went out. He cursed. He could not see where the door was situated. In his struggle he had quite lost his bearings. The strange beast, disturbed by the splutter of the match, began to move again. "Time!" called Woodhouse, with a sudden gleam of mirth, but the thing was not coming at him again. He must have hurt it, he thought, with the broken bottle. He felt a dull pain in his ankle. Probably he was bleeding there. He wondered if it would support him if he tried to stand up. The night outside was very still. There was no sound of any one moving. The sleepy fools had not heard those wings battering upon the dome, nor his shouts. It was no good wasting strength in shouting. The monster flapped its wings and startled him into a defensive attitude. He hit his elbow against the seat, and it fell over with a crash. He cursed this, and then he cursed the darkness.

Suddenly the oblong patch of starlight seemed to sway to and fro. Was he going to faint? It would never do to faint. He clenched his fists and set his teeth to hold himself together. Where had the door got to? It occurred to him he could get his bearings by the stars visible through the skylight. The patch of stars he saw was in Sagittarius and south-eastward; the door was north—or was it north by west? He tried to think. If he could get the door open he might retreat. It might be the thing was wounded. The suspense was beastly. "Look here!" he said, "if you don't come on, I shall come at you."

Then the thing began clambering up the side of the observatory, and he saw its black outline gradually blot out the skylight. Was it in retreat? He forgot about the door, and watched as the dome shifted and creaked. Somehow he did not feel very frightened or excited now. He felt a curious sinking sensation inside him. The sharply-defined patch of light, with the black form moving across it, seemed to be growing smaller and smaller. That was curious. He began to feel very thirsty, and yet he did not feel inclined to get anything to drink. He seemed to be sliding down a long funnel.

He felt a burning sensation in his throat, and then he perceived it was broad daylight, and that one of the Dyak servants was looking at him with a curious expression. Then there was the top of Thaddy's face upside down. Funny fellow, Thaddy, to go about like that! Then he grasped the situation better, and perceived that his head was on Thaddy's knee, and Thaddy was giving him brandy. And then he saw the eyepiece of the telescope with a lot of red smears on it. He began to remember.

"You've made this observatory in a pretty mess," said Thaddy.

The Dyak boy was beating up an egg in brandy. Woodhouse took this and sat up. He felt a sharp twinge of pain. His ankle was tied up, so were his arm and the side of his face. The smashed glass, red-stained, lay about the floor, the telescope seat was overturned, and by the opposite wall was a dark pool. The door was open, and he saw the grey summit of the mountain against a brilliant background of blue sky.

"Pah!" said Woodhouse. "Who's been killing calves here? Take me out of it."

Then he remembered the Thing, and the fight he had had with it.

"What *was* it?" he said to Thaddy—"The Thing I fought with?"

"*You* know that best," said Thaddy. "But, anyhow, don't worry yourself now about it. Have some more to drink."

Thaddy, however, was curious enough, and it was a hard struggle between duty and inclination to keep Woodhouse quiet until he was decently put away in bed, and had slept upon the copious dose of meat-extract Thaddy considered advisable. They then talked it over together.

"It was," said Woodhouse, "more like a big bat than anything else in the world. It had sharp, short ears, and soft fur, and its wings were leathery. Its teeth were little, but devilish sharp, and its jaw could not have been very strong or else it would have bitten through my ankle."

"It has pretty nearly," said Thaddy.

"It seemed to me to hit out with its claws pretty freely. That is about as much as I know about the beast. Our conversation was intimate, so to speak, and yet not confidential."

"The Dyak chaps talk about a Big Colugo, a Klang-utang—whatever that may be. It does not often attack man, but I suppose you made it nervous. They say there is a Big Colugo and a Little Colugo, and a something else that sounds like gobble. They all fly about at night. For my own part I know there are flying foxes and flying lemurs about here, but they are none of them very big beasts."

"There are more things in heaven and earth," said Woodhouse—and Thaddy groaned at the quotation—"and more particularly in the forests of Borneo, than are dreamt of in our philosophies. On the whole, if the Borneo fauna is going to disgorge any more of its novelties upon me, I should prefer that it did so when I was not occupied in the observatory at night and alone."

THE TRIUMPHS OF A TAXIDERMIST

Here are some of the secrets of taxidermy. They were told me by the taxidermist in a mood of elation. He told me them in the time between the first glass of whisky and the fourth, when a man is no longer cautious and yet not drunk. We sat in his den together; his library it was, his sitting and his eating-room—separated by a bead curtain, so far as the sense of sight went, from the noisome den where he plied his trade.

He sat on a deck chair, and when he was not tapping refractory bits of coal with them, he kept his feet—on which he wore, after the manner of sandals, the holy relics of a pair of carpet slippers—out of the way upon the mantel-piece, among the glass eyes. And his trousers, by-the-by—though they have nothing to do with his triumphs—were a most horrible yellow plaid, such as they made when our fathers wore side-whiskers and there were crinolines in the land. Further, his hair was black, his face rosy, and his eye a fiery brown; and his coat was chiefly of grease upon a basis of velveteen. And his pipe had a bowl of china showing the Graces, and his spectacles were always askew, the left eye glaring nakedly at you, small and penetrating; the right, seen through a glass darkly, magnified and mild. Thus his discourse ran: "There never was a man who could stuff like me, Bellows, never. I have stuffed elephants and I have stuffed moths, and the things have looked all the livelier and better for it. And I have stuffed human beings—chiefly amateur ornithologists. But I stuffed a nigger once.

"No, there is no law against it. I made him with all his fingers out and used him as a hat-rack, but that fool Homersby got up a quarrel with him late one night and spoilt him. That was before your time. It is hard to get skins, or I would have another.

"Unpleasant? I don't see it. Seems to me taxidermy is a promising third course to burial or cremation. You could keep all your dear ones by you. Bric-à-brac of that sort stuck about the house would be as good as most company, and much less expensive. You might have them fitted up with clockwork to do things.

"Of course they would have to be varnished, but they need not shine more than lots of people do naturally. Old Manningtree's bald head…. Anyhow, you could talk to them without interruption. Even aunts. There is a great future before taxidermy, depend upon it. There is fossils again…."

He suddenly became silent.

"No, I don't think I ought to tell you that." He sucked at his pipe thoughtfully. "Thanks, yes. Not too much water.

"Of course, what I tell you now will go no further. You know I have made some dodos and a great auk? No! Evidently you are an amateur at taxidermy. My dear fellow, half the great auks in the world are about as genuine as the handkerchief of Saint Veronica, as the Holy Coat of Treves. We make 'em of grebes' feathers and the like. And the great auk's eggs too!"

"Good heavens!"

"Yes, we make them out of fine porcelain. I tell you it is worth while. They fetch—one fetched £300 only the other day. That one was really genuine, I believe, but of course one is never certain. It is very fine work, and afterwards you have to get them dusty, for no one who owns one of these precious eggs has ever the temerity to clean the thing. That's the beauty of the business. Even if they suspect an egg they do not like to examine it too closely. It's such brittle capital at the best.

"You did not know that taxidermy rose to heights like that. My boy, it has risen higher. I have rivalled the hands of Nature herself. One of the *genuine* great auks"—his voice fell to a whisper—one of the *genuine* great auks *was made by me*."

"No. You must study ornithology, and find out which it is yourself. And what is more, I have been approached by a syndicate of dealers to stock one of the unexplored skerries to the north of Iceland with specimens. I may—some day. But I have another little thing in hand just now. Ever heard of the dinornis?

"It is one of those big birds recently extinct in New Zealand. 'Moa' is its common name, so called because extinct: there is no moa now. See? Well, they have got bones of it, and from some of the marshes even feathers and dried bits of skin. Now, I am going to—well, there is no need to make any bones about it—going to *forge* a complete stuffed moa. I know a chap out there who will pretend to make the find in a kind of antiseptic swamp, and say he stuffed it at once, as it threatened to fall to pieces. The feathers are peculiar, but I have got a simply lovely way of dodging up singed bits of ostrich plume. Yes, that is the new smell you noticed. They can only discover the fraud with a microscope, and they will hardly care to pull a nice specimen to bits for that.

"In this way, you see, I give my little push in the advancement of science.

"But all this is merely imitating Nature. I have done more than that in my time. I have—beaten her."

He took his feet down from the mantel-board, and leant over confidentially towards me. "I have *created* birds," he said in a low voice. "*New* birds. Improvements. Like no birds that was ever seen before."

He resumed his attitude during an impressive silence.

"Enrich the universe; *rath*-er. Some of the birds I made were new kinds of humming birds, and very beautiful little things, but some of them were simply rum. The rummest, I think, was the *Anomalopteryx Jejuna. Jejunus-a-um*—empty—so called because there was really nothing in it; a thoroughly empty bird—except for stuffing. Old Javvers has the thing now, and I suppose he is almost as proud of it as I am. It is a masterpiece, Bellows. It has all the silly clumsiness of your pelican, all the solemn want of dignity of your parrot, all the gaunt ungainliness of a flamingo, with all the extravagant chromatic conflict of a mandarin duck. *Such* a bird. I made it out of the skeletons of a stork and a toucan and a job lot of feathers. Taxidermy of that kind is just pure joy, Bellows, to a real artist in the art.

"How did I come to make it? Simple enough, as all great inventions are. One of those young genii who write us Science Notes in the papers got hold of a German pamphlet about the birds of New Zealand, and translated some of it by means of a dictionary and his mother-wit—he must have been one of a very large family with a small mother—and he got mixed between the living apteryx and the extinct anomalopteryx; talked about a bird five feet high, living in the jungles of the North Island, rare, shy, specimens difficult to obtain, and so on. Javvers, who even for a collector, is a miraculously ignorant man, read these paragraphs, and swore he would have the thing at any price. Raided the dealers with enquiries. It shows what a man can do by persistence—will-power. Here was a bird-collector swearing he would have a specimen of a bird that did not exist, that never had existed, and which for very shame of its own profane ungainliness, probably would not exist now if it could help itself. And he got it. *He got it.*"

"Have some more whisky, Bellows?" said the taxidermist, rousing himself from a transient contemplation of the mysteries of will-power and the collecting turn of mind. And, replenished, he proceeded to tell me of how he concocted a most attractive mermaid, and how an itinerant preacher, who could not get an audience because of it, smashed it because it was idolatry, or worse, at Burslem Wakes. But as the conversation of all the parties to this transaction, creator, would-be preserver, and destroyer, was uniformly unfit for publication, this cheerful incident must still remain unprinted.

The reader unacquainted with the dark ways of the collector may perhaps be inclined to doubt my taxidermist, but so far as great auks' eggs, and the bogus stuffed birds are concerned, I find that he has the confirmation of distinguished ornithological writers. And the note about the New Zealand bird certainly appeared in a morning paper of unblemished reputation, for the Taxidermist keeps a copy and has shown it to me.

A DEAL IN OSTRICHES

"Talking of the prices of birds, I've seen an ostrich that cost three hundred pounds," said the Taxidermist, recalling his youth of travel. "Three hundred pounds!"

He looked at me over his spectacles. "I've seen another that was refused at four."

"No," he said, "it wasn't any fancy points. They was just plain ostriches. A little off colour, too—owing to dietary. And there wasn't any particular restriction of the demand either. You'd have thought five ostriches would have ruled cheap on an East Indiaman. But the point was, one of 'em had swallowed a diamond.

"The chap it got it off was Sir Mohini Padishah, a tremendous swell, a Piccadilly swell you might say up to the neck of him, and then an ugly black head and a whopping turban, with this diamond in it. The blessed bird pecked suddenly and had it, and when the chap made a fuss it realised it had done wrong, I suppose, and went and mixed itself with the others to preserve its *incog*. It all happened in a minute. I was among the first to arrive, and there was this heathen going over his gods, and two sailors and the man who had charge of the birds laughing fit to split. It was a rummy way of losing a jewel, come to think of it. The man in charge hadn't been about just at the moment, so that he didn't know which bird it was. Clean lost, you see. I didn't feel half sorry, to tell you the truth. The beggar had been swaggering over his blessed diamond ever since he came aboard.

"A thing like that goes from stem to stern of a ship in no time. Every one was talking about it. Padishah went below to hide his feelings. At dinner—he pigged at a table by himself, him and two other Hindoos—the captain kind of jeered at him about it, and he got very excited. He turned round and talked into my ear. He would not buy the birds; he would have his diamond. He demanded his rights as a British subject. His diamond must be found. He was firm upon that. He would appeal to the House of Lords. The man in charge of the birds was one of those wooden-headed chaps you can't get a new idea into anyhow. He refused any proposal to interfere with the birds by way of medicine. His instructions were to feed them so-and-so and treat them so-and-so, and it was as much as his place was worth not to feed them so-and-so and treat them so-and-so. Padishah had wanted a stomach-pump—though you can't do that to a bird, you know. This Padishah was full of bad law, like most of these blessed Bengalis, and talked of having a lien on the birds, and so forth. But an old boy, who said his son was a London barrister, argued that what a bird swallowed became *ipso facto* part of the bird, and that Padishah's only remedy lay in an action for damages, and even then it might be possible to show contributory negligence. He hadn't any right of way about an ostrich that didn't belong to him. That upset Padishah extremely, the more so as most of us expressed an opinion that that was the reasonable view. There wasn't any lawyer aboard to settle the matter, so we all talked pretty free. At last, after Aden, it appears that he came round to the general opinion, and went privately to the man in charge and made an offer for all five ostriches.

"The next morning there was a fine shindy at breakfast. The man hadn't any authority to deal with the birds, and nothing on earth would induce him to sell; but it seems he told Padishah that a Eurasian named Potter had already made him an offer, and on that Padishah denounced Potter before us all. But I think the most of us thought it rather smart of Potter, and I know that when Potter said that he'd wired at Aden to London to buy the birds, and would have an answer at Suez, I cursed pretty richly at a lost opportunity.

"At Suez, Padishah gave way to tears—actual wet tears—when Potter became the owner of the birds, and offered him two hundred and fifty right off for the five, being more than two hundred per cent. on what Potter had given. Potter said he'd be hanged if he parted with a feather of them—that he meant to kill them off one by one and find the diamond; but afterwards, thinking it over, he relented a little. He was a gambling hound, was this Potter, a little queer at cards, and this kind of prize-packet business must have suited him down to the ground. Anyhow, he offered, for a lark, to sell the birds separately to separate people by auction at a starting price of £80 for a bird. But one of them, he said, he meant to keep for luck.

"You must understand this diamond was a valuable one—a little Jew chap, a diamond merchant, who was with us, had put it at three or four thousand when Padishah had shown it to him—and this idea of an ostrich gamble caught on. Now it happened that I'd been having a few talks on general subjects with the man who looked after these ostriches, and quite incidentally he'd said one of the birds was ailing, and he fancied it had indigestion. It had one feather in its tail almost all white, by which I knew it, and so when, next day, the auction started with it, I capped Padishah's eighty-five by ninety. I fancy I was a bit too sure and eager with my bid, and some of the others spotted the fact that I was in the know. And Padishah went for that particular bird like an irresponsible lunatic. At last the Jew diamond merchant got it for £175, and Padishah said £180 just after the hammer came down—so Potter declared. At any rate the Jew merchant secured it, and there and then he got a gun and shot it. Potter made a Hades of a fuss because he said it would injure the sale of the other three, and Padishah, of course, behaved like an idiot; but all of us were very much excited. I can tell you I was precious glad when that dissection was over, and no diamond had turned up—precious glad. I'd gone to one-forty on that particular bird myself.

"The little Jew was like most Jews—he didn't make any great fuss over bad luck; but Potter declined to go on with the auction until it was understood that the goods could not be delivered until the sale was over. The little Jew wanted to argue that the case was exceptional, and as the discussion ran pretty even, the thing was postponed until the next morning. We had a lively dinner-table that evening, I can tell you, but in the end Potter got his way, since it would stand to reason he would be safer if he stuck to all the birds, and that we owed him some consideration for his sportsmanlike behaviour. And the old gentleman whose son was a lawyer said he'd been thinking the thing over and that it was very doubtful if, when a bird had been opened and the diamond recovered, it ought not to be handed back to the proper owner. I remember I suggested it came under the laws of treasure-trove—which was really the truth of the matter. There was a hot argument, and we settled it was certainly foolish to kill the bird on board the ship. Then the old gentleman, going at large through his legal talk, tried to make out the sale was a lottery and illegal, and appealed to the captain; but Potter said he sold the birds *as* ostriches. He didn't want to sell any diamonds, he said, and didn't offer that as an inducement. The three birds he put up, to the best of his knowledge and belief, did *not* contain a diamond. It was in the one he kept—so he hoped.

"Prices ruled high next day all the same. The fact that now there were four chances instead of five of course caused a rise. The blessed birds averaged 227, and, oddly enough, this Padishah didn't secure one of 'em—not one. He made too much shindy, and when he ought to have been bidding he was talking about liens, and, besides, Potter was a bit down on him. One fell to a quiet little officer chap, another to the little Jew, and the third was syndicated by the engineers. And then Potter seemed suddenly sorry for having sold them, and said he'd flung away a clear thousand pounds, and that very likely he'd draw a blank and that he always had been a fool, but when I went and had a bit of a talk to him, with the idea of getting him to hedge on his last chance, I found he'd already sold the bird he'd reserved to a political chap that was on board, a chap who'd been studying Indian morals and social questions in his vacation. That last was the three hundred pounds bird. Well, they landed three of the blessed creatures at Brindisi—though the old gentleman said it was a breach of the Customs regulations—and Potter and Padishah landed too. The Hindoo seemed half mad as he saw his blessed diamond going this way and that, so to speak. He kept on saying he'd get an injunction—he had injunction on the brain—and giving his name and address to the chaps who'd bought the birds, so that they'd know where to send the diamond. None of them wanted his name and address, and none of them would give their own. It was a fine row I can tell you—on the platform. They all went off by different trains. I came on to Southampton, and there I saw the last of the birds, as I came ashore; it was the one the engineers bought, and it was standing up near the bridge, in a kind of crate, and looking as leggy and silly a setting for a valuable diamond as ever you saw—if it *was* a setting for a valuable diamond.

"*How did it end?* Oh! like that. Well—perhaps. Yes, there's one more thing that may throw light on it. A week or so after landing I was down Regent-street doing a bit of shopping, and who should I see arm-in-arm and having a purple time of it but Padishah and Potter. If you come to think of it—

"Yes. *I've* thought that. Only, you see, there's no doubt the diamond was real. And Padishah was an eminent Hindoo. I've seen his name in the papers—often. But whether the bird swallowed the diamond certainly is another matter, as you say."

THROUGH A WINDOW

After his legs were set, they carried Bailey into the study and put him on a couch before the open window. There he lay, a live—even a feverish man down to the loins, and below that a double-barrelled mummy swathed in white wrappings. He tried to read, even tried to write a little, but most of the time he looked out of the window.

He had thought the window cheerful to begin with, but now he thanked God for it many times a day. Within, the room was dim and grey, and in the reflected light the wear of the furniture showed plainly. His medicine and drink stood on the little table, with such litter as the bare branches of a bunch of grapes or the ashes of a cigar upon a green plate, or a day old evening paper. The view outside was flooded with light, and across the corner of it came the head of the acacia, and at the foot the top of the balcony-railing of hammered iron. In the foreground was the weltering silver of the river, never quiet and yet never tiresome. Beyond was the reedy bank, a broad stretch of meadow land, and then a dark line of trees ending in a group of poplars at the distant bend of the river, and, upstanding behind them, a square church tower.

Up and down the river, all day long, things were passing. Now a string of barges drifting down to London, piled with lime or barrels of beer; then a steam-launch, disengaging heavy masses of black smoke, and disturbing the whole width of the river with long rolling waves; then an impetuous electric launch, and then a boatload of pleasure-seekers, a solitary sculler, or a four from some rowing club. Perhaps the river was quietest of a morning or late at night. One moonlight night some people drifted down singing, and with a zither playing—it sounded very pleasantly across the water.

In a few days Bailey began to recognise some of the craft; in a week he knew the intimate history of half-a-dozen. The launch *Luzon*, from Fitzgibbon's, two miles up, would go fretting by, sometimes three or four times a day, conspicuous with its colouring of Indian-red and yellow, and its two Oriental attendants; and one day, to Bailey's vast amusement, the house-boat *Purple Emperor* came to a stop outside, and breakfasted in the most shameless domesticity. Then one afternoon, the captain of a slow-moving barge began a quarrel with his wife as they came into sight from the left, and had carried it to personal violence before he vanished behind the window-frame to the right. Bailey regarded all this as an entertainment got up to while away his illness, and applauded all the more moving incidents. Mrs Green, coming in at rare intervals with his meals, would catch him clapping his hands or softly crying, "Encore!" But the river players had other engagements, and his encore went unheeded.

"I should never have thought I could take such an interest in things that did not concern me," said Bailey to Wilderspin, who used to come in in his nervous, friendly way and try to comfort the sufferer by being talked to. "I thought this idle capacity was distinctive of little children and old maids. But it's just circumstances. I simply can't work, and things have to drift; it's no good to fret and struggle. And so I lie here and am as amused as a baby with a rattle, at this river and its affairs.

"Sometimes, of course, it gets a bit dull, but not often.

"I would give anything, Wilderspin, for a swamp—just one swamp—once. Heads swimming and a steam launch to the rescue, and a chap or so hauled out with a boat-hook…. There goes Fitzgibbon's launch! They have a new boat-hook, I see, and the little blackie is still in the dumps. I don't think he's very well, Wilderspin. He's been like that for two or three days, squatting sulky-fashion and meditating over the churning of the water. Unwholesome for him to be always staring at the frothy water running away from the stern."

They watched the little steamer fuss across the patch of sunlit river, suffer momentary occultation from the acacia, and glide out of sight behind the dark window-frame.

"I'm getting a wonderful eye for details," said Bailey: "I spotted that new boat-hook at once. The other nigger is a funny little chap. He never used to swagger with the old boat-hook like that."

"Malays, aren't they?" said Wilderspin.

"Don't know," said Bailey. "I thought one called all that sort of manner Lascar."

Then he began to tell Wilderspin what he knew of the private affairs of the houseboat, *Purple Emperor*. "Funny," he said, "how these people come from all points of the compass—from Oxford and Windsor, from Asia and Africa—and gather and pass opposite the window just to entertain me. One man floated out of the infinite the day before yesterday, caught one perfect crab opposite, lost and recovered a scull, and passed on again. Probably he will never come into my life again. So far as I am concerned, he has lived and had his little troubles, perhaps thirty—perhaps forty—years on the earth, merely to make an ass of himself for three minutes in front of my window. Wonderful thing, Wilderspin, if you come to think of it."

"Yes," said Wilderspin; "*isn't* it?"

A day or two after this Bailey had a brilliant morning. Indeed, towards the end of the affair, it became almost as exciting as any window show very well could be. We will, however, begin at the beginning.

Bailey was all alone in the house, for his housekeeper had gone into the town three miles away to pay bills, and the servant had her holiday. The morning began dull. A canoe went up about half-past nine, and later a boat-load of camping men came down. But this was mere margin. Things became cheerful about ten o'clock.

It began with something white fluttering in the remote distance where the three poplars marked the river bend. "Pocket-handkerchief," said Bailey, when he saw it "No. Too big! Flag perhaps."

However, it was not a flag, for it jumped about. "Man in whites running fast, and this way," said Bailey. "That's luck! But his whites are precious loose!"

Then a singular thing happened. There was a minute pink gleam among the dark trees in the distance, and a little puff of pale grey that began to drift and vanish eastward. The man in white jumped and continued running. Presently the report of the shot arrived.

"What the devil!" said Bailey. "Looks as if someone was shooting at him."

He sat up stiffly and stared hard. The white figure was coming along the pathway through the corn. "It's one of those niggers from the Fitzgibbon's," said Bailey; "or may I be hanged! I wonder why he keeps sawing with his arm."

Then three other figures became indistinctly visible against the dark background of the trees.

Abruptly on the opposite bank a man walked into the picture. He was black-bearded, dressed in flannels, had a red belt, and a vast grey felt hat. He walked, leaning very much forward and with his hands swinging before him. Behind him one could see the grass swept by the towing-rope of the boat he was dragging. He was steadfastly regarding the white figure that was hurrying through the corn. Suddenly he stopped. Then, with a peculiar gesture, Bailey could see that he began pulling in the tow-rope hand over hand. Over the water could be heard the voices of the people in the still invisible boat.

"What are you after, Hagshot?" said someone.

The individual with the red belt shouted something that was inaudible, and went on lugging in the rope, looking over his shoulder at the advancing white figure as he did so. He came down the bank, and the rope bent a lane among the reeds and lashed the water between his pulls.

Then just the bows of the boat came into view, with the towing-mast and a tall, fair-haired man standing up and trying to see over the bank. The boat bumped unexpectedly among the reeds, and the tall, fair-haired man disappeared suddenly, having apparently fallen back into the invisible part of the boat. There was a curse and some indistinct laughter. Hagshot did not laugh, but hastily clambered into the boat and pushed off. Abruptly the boat passed out of Bailey's sight.

But it was still audible. The melody of voices suggested that its occupants were busy telling each other what to do.

The running figure was drawing near the bank. Bailey could now see clearly that it was one of Fitzgibbon's Orientals, and began to realise what the sinuous thing the man carried in his hand might be. Three other men followed one another through the corn, and the foremost carried what was probably the gun. They were perhaps two hundred yards or more behind the Malay.

"It's a man hunt, by all that's holy!" said Bailey.

The Malay stopped for a moment and surveyed the bank to the right. Then he left the path, and, breaking through the corn, vanished in that direction. The three pursuers followed suit, and their heads and gesticulating arms above the corn, after a brief interval, also went out of Bailey's field of vision.

Bailey so far forgot himself as to swear. "Just as things were getting lively!" he said. Something like a woman's shriek came through the air. Then shouts, a howl, a dull whack upon the balcony outside that made Bailey jump, and then the report of a gun.

"This is precious hard on an invalid," said Bailey.

But more was to happen yet in his picture. In fact, a great deal more. The Malay appeared again, running now along the bank up stream. His stride had more swing and less pace in it than before. He was threatening someone ahead with the ugly krees he carried. The blade, Bailey noticed, was dull—it did not shine as steel should.

Then came the tall, fair man, brandishing a boat-hook, and after him three other men in boating costume, running clumsily with oars. The man with the grey hat and red belt was not with them. After an interval the three men with the gun reappeared, still in the corn, but now near the river bank. They emerged upon the towing-path, and hurried after the others. The opposite bank was left blank and desolate again.

The sick-room was disgraced by more profanity. "I would give my life to see the end of this," said Bailey. There were indistinct shouts up stream. Once they seemed to be coming nearer, but they disappointed him.

Bailey sat and grumbled. He was still grumbling when his eye caught something black and round among the waves. "Hullo!" he said. He looked narrowly and saw two triangular black bodies frothing every now and then about a yard in front of this.

He was still doubtful when the little band of pursuers came into sight again, and began to point to this floating object. They were talking eagerly. Then the man with the gun took aim.

"He's swimming the river, by George!" said Bailey.

The Malay looked round, saw the gun, and went under. He came up so close to Bailey's bank of the river that one of the bars of the balcony hid him for a moment. As he emerged the man with the gun fired. The Malay kept steadily onward—Bailey could see the wet hair on his forehead now and the krees between his teeth—and was presently hidden by the balcony.

This seemed to Bailey an unendurable wrong. The man was lost to him for ever now, so he thought. Why couldn't the brute have got himself decently caught on the opposite bank, or shot in the water?

"It's worse than Edwin Drood," said Bailey.

Over the river, too, things had become an absolute blank. All seven men had gone down stream again, probably to get the boat and follow across. Bailey listened and waited. There was silence. "Surely it's not over like this," said Bailey.

Five minutes passed—ten minutes. Then a tug with two barges went up stream. The attitudes of the men upon these were the attitudes of those who see nothing remarkable in earth, water, or sky. Clearly the whole affair had passed out of sight of the river. Probably the hunt had gone into the beech woods behind the house.

"Confound it!" said Bailey. "To be continued again, and no chance this time of the sequel. But this is hard on a sick man."

He heard a step on the staircase behind him and looking round saw the door open. Mrs Green came in and sat down, panting. She still had her bonnet on, her purse in her hand, and her little brown basket upon her arm. "Oh, there!" she said, and left Bailey to imagine the rest.

"Have a little whisky and water, Mrs Green, and tell me about it," said Bailey.

Sipping a little, the lady began to recover her powers of explanation.

One of those black creatures at the Fitzgibbon's had gone mad, and was running about with a big knife, stabbing people. He had killed a groom, and stabbed the under-butler, and almost cut the arm off a boating gentleman.

"Running amuck with a krees," said Bailey. "I thought that was it."

And he was hiding in the wood when she came through it from the town.

"What! Did he run after you?" asked Bailey, with a certain touch of glee in his voice.

"No, that was the horrible part of it," Mrs Green explained. She had been right through the woods and had *never known he was there*. It was only when she met young Mr Fitzgibbon carrying his gun in the shrubbery that she heard anything about it. Apparently, what upset Mrs Green was the lost opportunity for emotion. She was determined, however, to make the most of what was left her.

"To think he was there all the time!" she said, over and over again.

Bailey endured this patiently enough for perhaps ten minutes. At last he thought it advisable to assert himself. "It's twenty past one, Mrs Green," he said. "Don't you think it time you got me something to eat?"

This brought Mrs Green suddenly to her knees.

"Oh Lord, sir!" she said. "Oh! don't go making me go out of this room, sir, till I know he's caught. He might have got into the house, sir. He might be creeping, creeping, with that knife of his, along the passage this very—"

She broke off suddenly and glared over him at the window. Her lower jaw dropped. Bailey turned his head sharply.

For the space of half a second things seemed just as they were. There was the tree, the balcony, the shining river, the distant church tower. Then he noticed that the acacia was displaced about a foot to the right, and that it was quivering, and the leaves were rustling. The tree was shaken violently, and a heavy panting was audible.

In another moment a hairy brown hand had appeared and clutched the balcony railings, and in another the face of the Malay was peering through these at the man on the couch. His expression was an unpleasant grin, by reason of the krees he held between his teeth, and he was bleeding from an ugly wound in his cheek. His hair wet to drying stuck out like horns from his head. His body was bare save for the wet trousers that clung to him. Bailey's first impulse was to spring from the couch, but his legs reminded him that this was impossible.

By means of the balcony and tree the man slowly raised himself until he was visible to Mrs Green. With a choking cry she made for the door and fumbled with the handle.

Bailey thought swiftly and clutched a medicine bottle in either hand. One he flung, and it smashed against the acacia. Silently and deliberately, and keeping his bright eyes fixed on Bailey, the Malay clambered into the balcony. Bailey, still clutching his second bottle, but with a sickening, sinking feeling about his heart, watched first one leg come over the railing and then the other.

It was Bailey's impression that the Malay took about an hour to get his second leg over the rail. The period that elapsed before the sitting position was changed to a standing one seemed enormous—days, weeks, possibly a year or so. Yet Bailey had no clear impression of anything going on in his mind during that vast period, except a vague wonder at his inability to throw the second medicine bottle. Suddenly the Malay glanced over his shoulder. There was the crack of a rifle. He flung up his arms and came down upon the couch. Mrs Green began a dismal shriek that seemed likely to last until Doomsday. Bailey stared at the brown body with its shoulder blade driven in, that writhed painfully across his legs and rapidly staining and soaking the spotless bandages. Then he looked at the long krees, with the reddish streaks upon its blade, that lay an inch beyond the trembling brown fingers upon the floor. Then at Mrs Green, who had backed hard against the door and was staring at the body and shrieking in gusty outbursts as if she would wake the dead. And then the body was shaken by one last convulsive effort.

The Malay gripped the krees, tried to raise himself with his left hand, and collapsed. Then he raised his head, stared for a moment at Mrs Green, and twisting his face round looked at Bailey. With a gasping groan the dying man succeeded in clutching the bed clothes with his disabled hand, and by a violent effort, which hurt Bailey's legs exceedingly, writhed sideways towards what must be his last victim. Then something seemed released in Bailey's mind and he brought down the second bottle with all his strength on to the Malay's face. The krees fell heavily upon the floor.

"Easy with those legs," said Bailey, as young Fitzgibbon and one of the boating party lifted the body off him.

Young Fitzgibbon was very white in the face. "I didn't mean to kill him," he said.

"It's just as well," said Bailey.

THE TEMPTATION OF HARRINGAY

It is quite impossible to say whether this thing really happened. It depends entirely on the word of R.M. Harringay, who is an artist.

Following his version of the affair, the narrative deposes that Harringay went into his studio about ten o'clock to see what he could make of the head that he had been working at the day before. The head in question was that of an Italian organ-grinder, and Harringay thought—but was not quite sure—that the title would be the "Vigil." So far he is frank, and his narrative bears the stamp of truth. He had seen the man expectant for pennies, and with a promptness that suggested genius, had had him in at once.

"Kneel. Look up at that bracket," said Harringay. "As if you expected pennies."

"Don't *grin*!" said Harringay. "I don't want to paint your gums. Look as though you were unhappy."

Now, after a night's rest, the picture proved decidedly unsatisfactory. "It's good work," said Harringay. "That little bit in the neck … But."

He walked about the studio and looked at the thing from this point and from that. Then he said a wicked word. In the original the word is given.

"Painting," he says he said. "Just a painting of an organ-grinder—a mere portrait. If it was a live organ-grinder I wouldn't mind. But somehow I never make things alive. I wonder if my imagination is wrong." This, too, has a truthful air. His imagination *is* wrong.

"That creative touch! To take canvas and pigment and make a man—as Adam was made of red ochre! But this thing! If you met it walking about the streets you would know it was only a studio production. The little boys would tell it to 'Garnome and git frimed.' Some little touch … Well—it won't do as it is."

He went to the blinds and began to pull them down. They were made of blue holland with the rollers at the bottom of the window, so that you pull them down to get more light. He gathered his palette, brushes, and mahl stick from his table. Then he turned to the picture and put a speck of brown in the corner of the mouth; and shifted his attention thence to the pupil of the eye. Then he decided that the chin was a trifle too impassive for a vigil.

Presently he put down his impedimenta, and lighting a pipe surveyed the progress of his work. "I'm hanged if the thing isn't sneering at me," said Harringay, and he still believes it sneered.

The animation of the figure had certainly increased, but scarcely in the direction he wished. There was no mistake about the sneer. "Vigil of the Unbeliever," said Harringay. "Rather subtle and clever that! But the left eyebrow isn't cynical enough."

He went and dabbed at the eyebrow, and added a little to the lobe of the ear to suggest materialism. Further consideration ensued. "Vigil's off, I'm afraid," said Harringay. "Why not Mephistopheles? But that's a bit *too* common. 'A Friend of the Doge,'—not so seedy. The armour won't do, though. Too Camelot. How about a scarlet robe and call him 'One of the Sacred College'? Humour in that, and an appreciation of Middle Italian History."

"There's always Benvenuto Cellini," said Harringay; "with a clever suggestion of a gold cup in one corner. But that would scarcely suit the complexion."

He describes himself as babbling in this way in order to keep down an unaccountably unpleasant sensation of fear. The thing was certainly acquiring anything but a pleasing expression. Yet it was as certainly becoming far more of a living thing than it had been—if a sinister one—far more alive than anything he had ever painted before. "Call it 'Portrait of a Gentleman,'" said Harringay;—"A Certain Gentleman."

"Won't do," said Harringay, still keeping up his courage. "Kind of thing they call Bad Taste. That sneer will have to come out. That gone, and a little more fire in the eye—never noticed how warm his eye was before—and he might do for—? What price Passionate Pilgrim? But that devilish face won't do—*this* side of the Channel.

"Some little inaccuracy does it," he said; "eyebrows probably too oblique,"—therewith pulling the blind lower to get a better light, and resuming palette and brushes.

The face on the canvas seemed animated by a spirit of its own. Where the expression of diablerie came in he found impossible to discover. Experiment was necessary. The eyebrows—it could scarcely be the eyebrows? But he altered them. No, that was no better; in fact, if anything, a trifle more satanic. The corner of the mouth? Pah! more than ever a leer—and now, retouched, it was ominously grim. The eye, then? Catastrophe! he had filled his brush with vermilion instead of brown, and yet he had felt sure it was brown! The eye seemed now to have rolled in its socket, and was glaring at him an eye of fire. In a flash of passion, possibly with something of the courage of panic, he struck the brush full of bright red athwart the picture; and then a very curious thing, a very strange thing indeed, occurred—if it *did* occur.

The diabolified Italian before him shut both his eyes, pursed his mouth, and wiped the colour off his face with his hand.

Then the *red eye* opened again, with a sound like the opening of lips, and the face smiled. "That was rather hasty of you," said the picture.

Harringay states that, now that the worst had happened, his self-possession returned. He had a saving persuasion that devils were reasonable creatures.

"Why do you keep moving about then," he said, "making faces and all that—sneering and squinting, while I am painting you?"

"I don't," said the picture.

"You *do*," said Harringay.

"It's yourself," said the picture.

"It's *not* myself," said Harringay.

"It *is* yourself," said the picture. "No! don't go hitting me with paint again, because it's true. You have been trying to fluke an expression on my face all the morning. Really, you haven't an idea what your picture ought to look like."

"I have," said Harringay.

"You have *not*," said the picture: "You *never* have with your pictures. You always start with the vaguest presentiment of what you are going to do; it is to be something beautiful—you are sure of that—and devout, perhaps, or tragic; but beyond that it is all experiment and chance. My dear fellow! you don't think you can paint a picture like that?"

Now it must be remembered that for what follows we have only Harringay's word.

"I shall paint a picture exactly as I like," said Harringay, calmly.

This seemed to disconcert the picture a little. "You can't paint a picture without an inspiration," it remarked.

"But I *had* an inspiration—for this."

"Inspiration!" sneered the sardonic figure; "a fancy that came from your seeing an organ-grinder looking up at a window! Vigil! Ha, ha! You just started painting on the chance of something coming—that's what you did. And when I saw you at it I came. I want a talk with you!"

"Art, with you," said the picture,—"it's a poor business. You potter. I don't know how it is, but you don't seem able to throw your soul into it. You know too much. It hampers you. In the midst of your enthusiasms you ask yourself whether something like this has not been done before. And ..."

"Look here," said Harringay, who had expected something better than criticism from the devil. "Are you going to talk studio to me?" He filled his number twelve hoghair with red paint.

"The true artist," said the picture, "is always an ignorant man. An artist who theorises about his work is no longer artist but critic. Wagner ... I say!—What's that red paint for?"

"I'm going to paint you out," said Harringay. "I don't want to hear all that Tommy Rot. If you think just because I'm an artist by trade I'm going to talk studio to you, you make a precious mistake."

"One minute," said the picture, evidently alarmed. "I want to make you an offer—a genuine offer. It's right what I'm saying. You lack inspirations. Well. No doubt you've heard of the Cathedral of Cologne, and the Devil's Bridge, and—"

"Rubbish," said Harringay. "Do you think I want to go to perdition simply for the pleasure of painting a good picture, and getting it slated. Take that."

His blood was up. His danger only nerved him to action, so he says. So he planted a dab of vermilion in his creature's mouth. The Italian spluttered and tried to wipe it off—evidently horribly surprised. And then—according to Harringay—there began a very remarkable struggle, Harringay splashing away with the red paint, and the picture wriggling about and wiping it off as fast as he put it on. "*Two* masterpieces," said the demon. "Two indubitable masterpieces for a Chelsea artist's soul. It's a bargain?" Harringay replied with the paint brush.

For a few minutes nothing could be heard but the brush going and the spluttering and ejaculations of the Italian. A lot of the strokes he caught on his arm and hand, though Harringay got over his guard often enough. Presently the paint on the palette gave out and the two antagonists stood breathless, regarding each other. The picture was so smeared with red that it looked as if it had been rolling about a slaughterhouse, and it was painfully out of breath and very uncomfortable with the wet paint trickling down its neck. Still, the first round was in its favour on the whole. "Think," it said, sticking pluckily to its point, "two supreme master-pieces—in different styles. Each equivalent to the Cathedral..."

"*I* know," said Harringay, and rushed out of the studio and along the passage towards his wife's boudoir.

In another minute he was back with a large tin of enamel—Hedge Sparrow's Egg Tint, it was, and a brush. At the sight of that the artistic devil with the red eye began to scream. "*Three* masterpieces—culminating masterpieces."

Harringay delivered cut two across the demon, and followed with a thrust in the eye. There was an indistinct rumbling. "*Four* masterpieces," and a spitting sound.

But Harringay had the upper hand now and meant to keep it. With rapid, bold strokes he continued to paint over the writhing canvas, until at last it was a uniform field of shining Hedge Sparrow tint. Once the mouth reappeared and got as far as "Five master—" before he filled it with enamel; and near the end the red eye opened and glared at him indignantly. But at last nothing remained save a gleaming panel of drying enamel. For a little while a faint stirring beneath the surface puckered it slightly here and there, but presently even that died away and the thing was perfectly still.

Then Harringay—according to Harringay's account—lit his pipe and sat down and stared at the enamelled canvas, and tried to make out clearly what had happened. Then he walked round behind it, to see if the back of it was at all remarkable. Then it was he began to regret he had not photographed the Devil before he painted him out.

This is Harringay's story—not mine. He supports it by a small canvas (24 by 20) enamelled a pale green, and by violent asseverations. It is also true that he never has produced a masterpiece, and in the opinion of his intimate friends probably never will.

THE FLYING MAN

The Ethnologist looked at the *bhimraj* feather thoughtfully. "They seemed loth to part with it," he said.

"It is sacred to the Chiefs," said the lieutenant; "just as yellow silk, you know, is sacred to the Chinese Emperor."

The Ethnologist did not answer. He hesitated. Then opening the topic abruptly, "What on earth is this cock-and-bull story they have of a flying man?"

The lieutenant smiled faintly. "What did they tell you?"

"I see," said the Ethnologist, "that you know of your fame."

The lieutenant rolled himself a cigarette. "I don't mind hearing about it once more. How does it stand at present?"

"It's so confoundedly childish," said the Ethnologist, becoming irritated. "How did you play it off upon them?"

The lieutenant made no answer, but lounged back in his folding-chair, still smiling.

"Here am I, come four hundred miles out of my way to get what is left of the folk-lore of these people, before they are utterly demoralised by missionaries and the military, and all I find are a lot of impossible legends about a sandy-haired scrub of an infantry lieutenant. How he is invulnerable—how he can jump over elephants—how he can fly. That's the toughest nut. One old gentleman described your wings, said they had black plumage and were not quite as long as a mule. Said he often saw you by moonlight hovering over the crests out towards the Shendu country.—Confound it, man!"

The lieutenant laughed cheerfully. "Go on," he said. "Go on."

The Ethnologist did. At last he wearied. "To trade so," he said, "on these unsophisticated children of the mountains. How could you bring yourself to do it, man?"

"I'm sorry," said the lieutenant, "but truly the thing was forced upon me. I can assure you I was driven to it. And at the time I had not the faintest idea of how the Chin imagination would take it. Or curiosity. I can only plead it was an indiscretion and not malice that made me replace the folk-lore by a new legend. But as you seem aggrieved, I will try and explain the business to you.

"It was in the time of the last Lushai expedition but one, and Walters thought these people you have been visiting were friendly. So, with an airy confidence in my capacity for taking care of myself, he sent me up the gorge—fourteen miles of it—with three of the Derbyshire men and half a dozen Sepoys, two mules, and his blessing, to see what popular feeling was like at that village you visited. A force of ten—not counting the mules—fourteen miles, and during a war! You saw the road?"

"*Road*!" said the Ethnologist.

"It's better now than it was. When we went up we had to wade in the river for a mile where the valley narrows, with a smart stream frothing round our knees and the stones as slippery as ice. There it was I dropped my rifle. Afterwards the Sappers blasted the cliff with dynamite and made the convenient way you came by. Then below, where those very high cliffs come, we had to keep on dodging across the river—I should say we crossed it a dozen times in a couple of miles.

"We got in sight of the place early the next morning. You know how it lies, on a spur halfway between the big hills, and as we began to appreciate how wickedly quiet the village lay under the sunlight, we came to a stop to consider.

"At that they fired a lump of filed brass idol at us, just by way of a welcome. It came twanging down the slope to the right of us where the boulders are, missed my shoulder by an inch or so, and plugged the mule that carried all the provisions and utensils. I never heard such a death-rattle before or since. And at that we became aware of a number of gentlemen carrying matchlocks, and dressed in things like plaid dusters, dodging about along the neck between the village and the crest to the east.

"'Right about face,' I said. 'Not too close together.'

"And with that encouragement my expedition of ten men came round and set off at a smart trot down the valley again hitherward. We did not wait to save anything our dead had carried, but we kept the second mule with us—he carried my tent and some other rubbish—out of a feeling of friendship.

"So ended the battle—ingloriously. Glancing back, I saw the valley dotted with the victors, shouting and firing at us. But no one was hit. These Chins and their guns are very little good except at a sitting shot. They will sit and finick over a boulder for hours taking aim, and when they fire running it is chiefly for stage effect. Hooker, one of the Derbyshire men, fancied himself rather with the rifle, and stopped behind for half a minute to try his luck as we turned the bend. But he got nothing.

"I'm not a Xenophon to spin much of a yarn about my retreating army. We had to pull the enemy up twice in the next two miles when he became a bit pressing, by exchanging shots with him, but it was a fairly monotonous affair—hard breathing chiefly—until we got near the place where the hills run in towards the river and pinch the valley into a gorge. And there we very luckily caught a glimpse of half a dozen round black heads coming slanting-ways over the hill to the left of us—the east that is—and almost parallel with us.

"At that I called a halt. 'Look here,' says I to Hooker and the other Englishmen; 'what are we to do now?' and I pointed to the heads.

"'Headed orf, or I'm a nigger,' said one of the men.

"'We shall be,' said another. 'You know the Chin way, George?'

"'They can pot every one of us at fifty yards,' says Hooker, 'in the place where the river is narrow. It's just suicide to go on down.'

"I looked at the hill to the right of us. It grew steeper lower down the valley, but it still seemed climbable. And all the Chins we had seen hitherto had been on the other side of the stream.

"'It's that or stopping,' says one of the Sepoys.

"So we started slanting up the hill. There was something faintly suggestive of a road running obliquely up the face of it, and that we followed. Some Chins presently came into view up the valley, and I heard some shots. Then I saw one of the Sepoys was sitting down about thirty yards below us. He had simply sat down without a word, apparently not wishing to give trouble. At that I called a halt again; I told Hooker to try another shot, and went back and found the man was hit in the leg. I took him up, carried him along to put him on the mule—already pretty well laden with the tent and other things which we had no time to take off. When I got up to the rest with him, Hooker had his empty Martini in his hand, and was grinning and pointing to a motionless black spot up the valley. All the rest of the Chins were behind boulders or back round the bend. 'Five hundred yards,' says Hooker, 'if an inch. And I'll swear I hit him in the head.'

"I told him to go and do it again, and with that we went on again.

"Now the hillside kept getting steeper as we pushed on, and the road we were following more and more of a shelf. At last it was mere cliff above and below us. 'It's the best road I have seen yet in Chin Lushai land,' said I to encourage the men, though I had a fear of what was coming.

"And in a few minutes the way bent round a corner of the cliff. Then, finis! the ledge came to an end.

"As soon as he grasped the position one of the Derbyshire men fell a-swearing at the trap we had fallen into. The Sepoys halted quietly. Hooker grunted and re-loaded, and went back to the bend.

"Then two of the Sepoy chaps helped their comrade down and began to un-load the mule.

"Now, when I came to look about me, I began to think we had not been so very unfortunate after all. We were on a shelf perhaps ten yards across it at widest. Above it the cliff projected so that we could not be shot down upon, and below was an almost sheer precipice of perhaps two or three hundred feet. Lying down we were invisible to anyone across the ravine. The only approach was along the ledge, and on that one man was as good as a host. We were in a natural stronghold, with only one disadvantage, our sole provision against hunger and thirst was one live mule. Still we were at most eight or nine miles from the main expedition, and no doubt, after a day or so, they would send up after us if we did not return.

"After a day or so ..."

The lieutenant paused. "Ever been thirsty, Graham?"

"Not that kind," said the Ethnologist.

"H'm. We had the whole of that day, the night, and the next day of it, and only a trifle of dew we wrung out of our clothes and the tent. And below us was the river going giggle, giggle, round a rock in mid stream. I never knew such a barrenness of incident, or such a quantity of sensation. The sun might have had Joshua's command still upon it for all the motion one could see; and it blazed like a near furnace. Towards the evening of the first day one of the Derbyshire men said something—nobody heard what—and went off round the bend of the cliff. We heard shots, and when Hooker looked round the corner he was gone. And in the morning the Sepoy whose leg was shot was in delirium, and jumped or fell over the cliff. Then we took the mule and shot it, and that must needs go over the cliff too in its last struggles, leaving eight of us.

"We could see the body of the Sepoy down below, with the head in the water. He was lying face downwards, and so far as I could make out was scarcely smashed at all. Badly as the Chins might covet his head, they had the sense to leave it alone until the darkness came.

"At first we talked of all the chances there were of the main body hearing the firing, and reckoned whether they would begin to miss us, and all that kind of thing, but we dried up as the evening came on. The Sepoys played games with bits of stone among themselves, and afterwards told stories. The night was rather chilly. The second day nobody spoke. Our lips were black and our throats afire, and we lay about on the ledge and glared at one another. Perhaps it's as well we kept our thoughts to ourselves. One of the British soldiers began writing some blasphemous rot on the rock with a bit of pipeclay, about his last dying will, until I stopped it. As I looked over the edge down into the valley and saw the river rippling I was nearly tempted to go after the Sepoy. It seemed a pleasant and desirable thing to go rushing down through the air with something to drink—or no more thirst at any rate—at the bottom. I remembered in time, though, that I was the officer in command, and my duty to set a good example, and that kept me from any such foolishness.

"Yet, thinking of that, put an idea into my head. I got up and looked at the tent and tent ropes, and wondered why I had not thought of it before. Then I came and peered over the cliff again. This time the height seemed greater and the pose of the Sepoy rather more painful. But it was that or nothing. And to cut it short, I parachuted.

"I got a big circle of canvas out of the tent, about three times the size of that table-cover, and plugged the hole in the centre, and I tied eight ropes round it to meet in the middle and make a parachute. The other chaps lay about and watched me as though they thought it was a new kind of delirium. Then I explained my notion to the two British soldiers and how I meant to do it, and as soon as the short dusk had darkened into night, I risked it. They held the thing high up, and I took a run the whole length of the ledge. The thing filled with air like a sail, but at the edge I will confess I funked and pulled up.

"As soon as I stopped I was ashamed of myself—as well I might be in front of privates—and went back and started again. Off I jumped this time—with a kind of sob, I remember—clean into the air, with the big white sail bellying out above me.

"I must have thought at a frightful pace. It seemed a long time before I was sure that the thing meant to keep steady. At first it heeled sideways. Then I noticed the face of the rock which seemed to be streaming up past me, and me motionless. Then I looked down and saw in the darkness the river and the dead Sepoy rushing up towards me. But in the indistinct light I also saw three Chins, seemingly aghast at the sight of me, and that the Sepoy was decapitated. At that I wanted to go back again.

"Then my boot was in the mouth of one, and in a moment he and I were in a heap with the canvas fluttering down on the top of us. I fancy I dashed out his brains with my foot. I expected nothing more than to be brained myself by the other two, but the poor heathen had never heard of Baldwin, and incontinently bolted.

"I struggled out of the tangle of dead Chin and canvas, and looked round. About ten paces off lay the head of the Sepoy staring in the moonlight. Then I saw the water and went and drank. There wasn't a sound in the world but the footsteps of the departing Chins, a faint shout from above, and the gluck of the water. So soon as I had drunk my full I started off down the river.

"That about ends the explanation of the flying man story. I never met a soul the whole eight miles of the way. I got to Walters' camp by ten o'clock, and a born idiot of a sentinel had the cheek to fire at me as I came trotting out of the darkness. So soon as I had hammered my story into Winter's thick skull, about fifty men started up the valley to clear the Chins out and get our men down. But for my own part I had too good a thirst to provoke it by going with them.

"You have heard what kind of a yarn the Chins made of it. Wings as long as a mule, eh?—And black feathers! The gay lieutenant bird! Well, well."

The lieutenant meditated cheerfully for a moment. Then he added, "You would scarcely credit it, but when they got to the ridge at last, they found two more of the Sepoys had jumped over."

"The rest were all right?" asked the Ethnologist.

"Yes," said the lieutenant; "the rest were all right, barring a certain thirst, you know."

And at the memory he helped himself to soda and whisky again.

THE DIAMOND MAKER

Some business had detained me in Chancery Lane until nine in the evening, and thereafter, having some inkling of a headache, I was disinclined either for entertainment or further work. So much of the sky as the high cliffs of that narrow cañon of traffic left visible spoke of a serene night, and I determined to make my way down to the Embankment, and rest my eyes and cool my head by watching the variegated lights upon the river. Beyond comparison the night is the best time for this place; a merciful darkness hides the dirt of the waters, and the lights of this transition age, red, glaring orange, gas-yellow, and electric white, are set in shadowy outlines of every possible shade between grey and deep purple. Through the arches of Waterloo Bridge a hundred points of light mark the sweep of the Embankment, and above its parapet rise the towers of Westminster, warm grey against the starlight. The black river goes by with only a rare ripple breaking its silence, and disturbing the reflections of the lights that swim upon its surface.

"A warm night," said a voice at my side.

I turned my head, and saw the profile of a man who was leaning over the parapet beside me. It was a refined face, not unhandsome, though pinched and pale enough, and the coat collar turned up and pinned round the throat marked his status in life as sharply as a uniform. I felt I was committed to the price of a bed and breakfast if I answered him.

I looked at him curiously. Would he have anything to tell me worth the money, or was he the common incapable—incapable even of telling his own story? There was a quality of intelligence in his forehead and eyes, and a certain tremulousness in his nether lip that decided me.

"Very warm," said I; "but not too warm for us here."

"No," he said, still looking across the water, "it is pleasant enough here … just now."

"It is good," he continued after a pause, "to find anything so restful as this in London. After one has been fretting about business all day, about getting on, meeting obligations, and parrying dangers, I do not know what one would do if it were not for such pacific corners." He spoke with long pauses between the sentences. "You must know a little of the irksome labour of the world, or you would not be here. But I doubt if you can be so brain-weary and footsore as I am … Bah! Sometimes I doubt if the game is worth the candle. I feel inclined to throw the whole thing over—name, wealth, and position—and take to some modest trade. But I know if I abandoned my ambition—hardly as she uses me—I should have nothing but remorse left for the rest of my days."

He became silent. I looked at him in astonishment. If ever I saw a man hopelessly hard-up it was the man in front of me. He was ragged and he was dirty, unshaven and unkempt; he looked as though he had been left in a dust-bin for a week. And he was talking to *me* of the irksome worries of a large business. I almost laughed outright. Either he was mad or playing a sorry jest on his own poverty.

"If high aims and high positions," said I, "have their drawbacks of hard work and anxiety, they have their compensations. Influence, the power of doing good, of assisting those weaker and poorer than ourselves; and there is even a certain gratification in display...."

My banter under the circumstances was in very vile taste. I spoke on the spur of the contrast of his appearance and speech. I was sorry even while I was speaking.

He turned a haggard but very composed face upon me. Said he: "I forget myself. Of course you would not understand."

He measured me for a moment. "No doubt it is very absurd. You will not believe me even when I tell you, so that it is fairly safe to tell you. And it will be a comfort to tell someone. I really have a big business in hand, a very big business. But there are troubles just now. The fact is ... I make diamonds."

"I suppose," said I, "you are out of work just at present?"

"I am sick of being disbelieved," he said impatiently, and suddenly unbuttoning his wretched coat he pulled out a little canvas bag that was hanging by a cord round his neck. From this he produced a brown pebble. "I wonder if you know enough to know what that is?" He handed it to me.

Now, a year or so ago, I had occupied my leisure in taking a London science degree, so that I have a smattering of physics and mineralogy. The thing was not unlike an uncut diamond of the darker sort, though far too large, being almost as big as the top of my thumb. I took it, and saw it had the form of a regular octahedron, with the curved faces peculiar to the most precious of minerals. I took out my penknife and tried to scratch it—vainly. Leaning forward towards the gaslamp, I tried the thing on my watch-glass, and scored a white line across that with the greatest ease.

I looked at my interlocutor with rising curiosity. "It certainly is rather like a diamond. But, if so, it is a Behemoth of diamonds. Where did you get it?"

"I tell you I made it," he said. "Give it back to me."

He replaced it hastily and buttoned his jacket. "I will sell it you for one hundred pounds," he suddenly whispered eagerly. With that my suspicions returned. The thing might, after all, be merely a lump of that almost equally hard substance, corundum, with an accidental resemblance in shape to the diamond. Or if it was a diamond, how came he by it, and why should he offer it at a hundred pounds?

We looked into one another's eyes. He seemed eager, but honestly eager. At that moment I believed it was a diamond he was trying to sell. Yet I am a poor man, a hundred pounds would leave a visible gap in my fortunes and no sane man would buy a diamond by gaslight from a ragged tramp on his personal warranty only. Still, a diamond that size conjured up a vision of many thousands of pounds. Then, thought I, such a stone could scarcely exist without being mentioned in every book on gems, and again I called to mind the stories of contraband and light-fingered Kaffirs at the Cape. I put the question of purchase on one side.

"How did you get it?" said I.

"I made it."

I had heard something of Moissan, but I knew his artificial diamonds were very small. I shook my head.

"You seem to know something of this kind of thing. I will tell you a little about myself. Perhaps then you may think better of the purchase." He turned round with his back to the river, and put his hands in his pockets. He sighed. "I know you will not believe me."

"Diamonds," he began—and as he spoke his voice lost its faint flavour of the tramp and assumed something of the easy tone of an educated man—"are to be made by throwing carbon out of combination in a suitable flux and under a suitable pressure; the carbon crystallises out, not as black-lead or charcoal-powder, but as small diamonds. So much has been known to chemists for years, but no one yet has hit upon exactly the right flux in which to melt up the carbon, or exactly the right pressure for the best results. Consequently the diamonds made by chemists are small and dark, and worthless as jewels. Now I, you know, have given up my life to this problem—given my life to it.

"I began to work at the conditions of diamond making when I was seventeen, and now I am thirty-two. It seemed to me that it might take all the thought and energies of a man for ten years, or twenty years, but, even if it did, the game was still worth the candle. Suppose one to have at last just hit the right trick, before the secret got out and diamonds became as common as coal, one might realise millions. Millions!"

He paused and looked for my sympathy. His eyes shone hungrily. "To think," said he, "that I am on the verge of it all, and here!

"I had," he proceeded, "about a thousand pounds when I was twenty-one, and this, I thought, eked out by a little teaching, would keep my researches going. A year or two was spent in study, at Berlin chiefly, and then I continued on my own account. The trouble was the secrecy. You see, if once I had let out what I was doing, other men might have been spurred on by my belief in the practicability of the idea; and I do not pretend to be such a genius as to have been sure of coming in first, in the case of a race for the discovery. And you see it was important that if I really meant to make a pile, people should not know it was an artificial process and capable of turning out diamonds by the ton. So I had to work all alone. At first I had a little laboratory, but as my resources began to run out I had to conduct my experiments in a wretched unfurnished room in Kentish Town, where I slept at last on a straw mattress on the floor among all my apparatus. The money simply flowed away. I grudged myself everything except scientific appliances. I tried to keep things going by a little teaching, but I am not a very good teacher, and I have no university degree, nor very much education except in chemistry, and I found I had to give a lot of time and labour for precious little money. But I got nearer and nearer the thing. Three years ago I settled the problem of the composition of the flux, and got near the pressure by putting this flux of mine and a certain carbon composition into a closed-up gun-barrel, filling up with water, sealing tightly, and heating."

He paused.

"Rather risky," said I.

"Yes. It burst, and smashed all my windows and a lot of my apparatus; but I got a kind of diamond powder nevertheless. Following out the problem of getting a big pressure upon the molten mixture from which the things were to crystallise, I hit upon some researches of Daubrée's at the Paris *Laboratorie des Poudres et Salpêtres*. He exploded dynamite in a tightly screwed steel cylinder, too strong to burst, and I found he could crush rocks into a muck not unlike the South African bed in which diamonds are found. It was a tremendous strain on my resources, but I got a steel cylinder made for my purpose after his pattern. I put in all my stuff and my explosives, built up a fire in my furnace, put the whole concern in, and—went out for a walk."

I could not help laughing at his matter-of-fact manner. "Did you not think it would blow up the house? Were there other people in the place?"

"It was in the interest of science," he said, ultimately. "There was a costermonger family on the floor below, a begging-letter writer in the room behind mine, and two flower-women were upstairs. Perhaps it was a bit thoughtless. But possibly some of them were out.

"When I came back the thing was just where I left it, among the white-hot coals. The explosive hadn't burst the case. And then I had a problem to face. You know time is an important element in crystallisation. If you hurry the process the crystals are small—it is only by prolonged standing that they grow to any size. I resolved to let this apparatus cool for two years, letting the temperature go down slowly during that time. And I was now quite out of money; and with a big fire and the rent of my room, as well as my hunger to satisfy, I had scarcely a penny in the world.

"I can hardly tell you all the shifts I was put to while I was making the diamonds. I have sold newspapers, held horses, opened cab-doors. For many weeks I addressed envelopes. I had a place as assistant to a man who owned a barrow, and used to call down one side of the road while he called down the other. Once for a week I had absolutely nothing to do, and I begged. What a week that was! One day the fire was going out and I had eaten nothing all day, and a little chap taking his girl out, gave me sixpence—to show-off. Thank heaven for vanity! How the fish-shops smelt! But I went and spent it all on coals, and had the furnace bright red again, and then—Well, hunger makes a fool of a man.

"At last, three weeks ago, I let the fire out. I took my cylinder and unscrewed it while it was still so hot that it punished my hands, and I scraped out the crumbling lava-like mass with a chisel, and hammered it into a powder upon an iron plate. And I found three big diamonds and five small ones. As I sat on the floor hammering, my door opened, and my neighbour, the begging-letter writer, came in. He was drunk—as he usually is. ''Nerchist,' said he. 'You're drunk,' said I. ''Structive scoundrel,' said he. 'Go to your father,' said I, meaning the Father of Lies. 'Never you mind,' said he, and gave me a cunning wink, and hiccuped, and leaning up against the door, with his other eye against the door-post, began to babble of how he had been prying in my room, and how he had gone to the police that morning, and how they had taken down everything he had to say—''siffiwas a ge'm,' said he. Then I suddenly realised I was in a hole. Either I should have to tell these police my little secret, and get the whole thing blown upon, or be lagged as an Anarchist. So I went up to my neighbour and took him by the collar, and rolled him about a bit, and then I gathered up my diamonds and cleared out. The evening newspapers called my den the Kentish-Town Bomb Factory. And now I cannot part with the things for love or money.

"If I go in to respectable jewellers they ask me to wait, and go and whisper to a clerk to fetch a policeman, and then I say I cannot wait. And I found out a receiver of stolen goods, and he simply stuck to the one I gave him and told me to prosecute if I wanted it back. I am going about now with several hundred thousand pounds-worth of diamonds round my neck, and without either food or shelter. You are the first person I have taken into my confidence. But I like your face and I am hard-driven."

He looked into my eyes.

"It would be madness," said I, "for me to buy a diamond under the circumstances. Besides, I do not carry hundreds of pounds about in my pocket. Yet I more than half believe your story. I will, if you like, do this: come to my office to-morrow...."

"You think I am a thief!" said he keenly. "You will tell the police. I am not coming into a trap."

"Somehow I am assured you are no thief. Here is my card. Take that, anyhow. You need not come to any appointment. Come when you will."

He took the card, and an earnest of my good-will.

"Think better of it and come," said I.

He shook his head doubtfully. "I will pay back your half-crown with interest some day—such interest as will amaze you," said he. "Anyhow, you will keep the secret?... Don't follow me."

He crossed the road and went into the darkness towards the little steps under the archway leading into Essex Street, and I let him go. And that was the last I ever saw of him.

Afterwards I had two letters from him asking me to send bank-notes—not cheques—to certain addresses. I weighed the matter over, and took what I conceived to be the wisest course. Once he called upon me when I was out. My urchin described him as a very thin, dirty, and ragged man, with a dreadful cough. He left no message. That was the finish of him so far as my story goes. I wonder sometimes what has become of him. Was he an ingenious monomaniac, or a fraudulent dealer in pebbles, or has he really made diamonds as he asserted? The latter is just sufficiently credible to make me think at times that I have missed the most brilliant opportunity of my life. He may of course be dead, and his diamonds carelessly thrown aside—one, I repeat, was almost as big as my thumb. Or he may be still wandering about trying to sell the things. It is just possible he may yet emerge upon society, and, passing athwart my heavens in the serene altitude sacred to the wealthy and the well-advertised, reproach me silently for my want of enterprise. I sometimes think I might at least have risked five pounds.

AEPYORNIS ISLAND

The man with the scarred face leant over the table and looked at my bundle.

"Orchids?" he asked.

"A few," I said.

"Cypripediums," he said.

"Chiefly," said I.

"Anything new? I thought not. *I* did these islands twenty-five—twenty-seven years ago. If you find anything new here—well it's brand new. I didn't leave much."

"I'm not a collector," said I.

"I was young then," he went on. "Lord! how I used to fly round." He seemed to take my measure. "I was in the East Indies two years, and in Brazil seven. Then I went to Madagascar."

"I know a few explorers by name," I said, anticipating a yarn. "Whom did you collect for?"

"Dawsons. I wonder if you've heard the name of Butcher ever?"

"Butcher—Butcher?" The name seemed vaguely present in my memory; then I recalled *Butcher* v. *Dawson*. "Why!" said I, "you are the man who sued them for four years' salary—got cast away on a desert island ..."

"Your servant," said the man with the scar, bowing. "Funny case, wasn't it? Here was me, making a little fortune on that island, doing nothing for it neither, and them quite unable to give me notice. It often used to amuse me thinking over it while I was there. I did calculations of it—big—all over the blessed atoll in ornamental figuring."

"How did it happen?" said I. "I don't rightly remember the case."

"Well.... You've heard of the Aepyornis?"

"Rather. Andrews was telling me of a new species he was working on only a month or so ago. Just before I sailed. They've got a thigh bone, it seems, nearly a yard long. Monster the thing must have been!"

"I believe you," said the man with the scar. "It *was* a monster. Sinbad's roc was just a legend of 'em. But when did they find these bones?"

"Three or four years ago—'91, I fancy. Why?"

"Why? Because *I* found 'em—Lord!—it's nearly twenty years ago. If Dawsons hadn't been silly about that salary they might have made a perfect ring in 'em.... *I* couldn't help the infernal boat going adrift."

He paused, "I suppose it's the same place. A kind of swamp about ninety miles north of Antananarivo. Do you happen to know? You have to go to it along the coast by boats. You don't happen to remember, perhaps?"

"I don't. I fancy Andrews said something about a swamp."

"It must be the same. It's on the east coast. And somehow there's something in the water that keeps things from decaying. Like creosote it smells. It reminded me of Trinidad. Did they get any more eggs? Some of the eggs I found were a foot-and-a-half long. The swamp goes circling round, you know, and cuts off this bit. It's mostly salt, too. Well.... What a time I had of it! I found the things quite by accident. We went for eggs, me and two native chaps, in one of those rum canoes all tied together, and found the bones at the same time. We had a tent and provisions for four days, and we pitched on one of the firmer places. To think of it brings that odd tarry smell back even now. It's funny work. You go probing into the mud with iron rods, you know. Usually the egg gets smashed. I wonder how long it is since these Aepyornises really lived. The missionaries say the natives have legends about when they were alive, but I never heard any such stories myself.[1] But certainly those eggs we got were as fresh as if they had been new laid. Fresh! Carrying them down to the boat one of my nigger chaps dropped one on a rock and it smashed. How I lammed into the beggar! But sweet it was, as if it was new laid, not even smelly, and its mother dead these four hundred years, perhaps. Said a centipede had bit him. However, I'm getting off the straight with the story. It had taken us all day to dig into the slush and get these eggs out unbroken, and we were all covered with beastly black mud, and naturally I was cross. So far as I knew they were the only eggs that have ever been got out not even cracked. I went afterwards to see the ones they have at the Natural History Museum in London; all of them were cracked and just stuck together like a mosaic, and bits missing. Mine were perfect, and I meant to blow them when I got back. Naturally I was annoyed at the silly duffer dropping three hours' work just on account of a centipede. I hit him about rather."

The man with the scar took out a clay pipe. I placed my pouch before him. He filled up absent-mindedly.

"How about the others? Did you get those home? I don't remember—"

"That's the queer part of the story. I had three others. Perfectly fresh eggs. Well, we put 'em in the boat, and then I went up to the tent to make some coffee, leaving my two heathens down by the beach—the one fooling about with his sting and the other helping him. It never occurred to me that the beggars would take advantage of the peculiar position I was in to pick a quarrel. But I suppose the centipede poison and the kicking I had given him had upset the one—he was always a cantankerous sort—and he persuaded the other.

---

[1] No European is known to have seen a live Aepyornis, with the doubtful exception of MacAndrew, who visited Madagascar in 1745.—H.G.W.

"I remember I was sitting and smoking and boiling up the water over a spirit-lamp business I used to take on these expeditions. Incidentally I was admiring the swamp under the sunset. All black and blood-red it was, in streaks—a beautiful sight. And up beyond the land rose grey and hazy to the hills, and the sky behind them red, like a furnace mouth. And fifty yards behind the back of me was these blessed heathen—quite regardless of the tranquil air of things—plotting to cut off with the boat and leave me all alone with three days' provisions and a canvas tent, and nothing to drink whatsoever, beyond a little keg of water. I heard a kind of yelp behind me, and there they were in this canoe affair—it wasn't properly a boat—and, perhaps, twenty yards from land. I realised what was up in a moment. My gun was in the tent, and, besides, I had no bullets—only duck shot. They knew that. But I had a little revolver in my pocket, and I pulled that out as I ran down to the beach.

"'Come back!' says I, flourishing it.

"They jabbered something at me, and the man that broke the egg jeered. I aimed at the other—because he was unwounded and had the paddle, and I missed. They laughed. However, I wasn't beat. I knew I had to keep cool, and I tried him again and made him jump with the whang of it. He didn't laugh that time. The third time I got his head, and over he went, and the paddle with him. It was a precious lucky shot for a revolver. I reckon it was fifty yards. He went right under. I don't know if he was shot, or simply stunned and drowned. Then I began to shout to the other chap to come back, but he huddled up in the canoe and refused to answer. So I fired out my revolver at him and never got near him.

"I felt a precious fool, I can tell you. There I was on this rotten, black beach, flat swamp all behind me, and the flat sea, cold after the sunset, and just this black canoe drifting steadily out to sea. I tell you I damned Dawsons and Jamrachs and Museums and all the rest of it just to rights. I bawled to this nigger to come back, until my voice went up into a scream.

"There was nothing for it but to swim after him and take my luck with the sharks. So I opened my clasp-knife and put it in my mouth, and took off my clothes and waded in. As soon as I was in the water I lost sight of the canoe, but I aimed, as I judged, to head it off. I hoped the man in it was too bad to navigate it, and that it would keep on drifting in the same direction. Presently it came up over the horizon again to the south-westward about. The afterglow of sunset was well over now and the dim of night creeping up. The stars were coming through the blue. I swum like a champion, though my legs and arms were soon aching.

"However, I came up to him by the time the stars were fairly out. As it got darker I began to see all manner of glowing things in the water—phosphorescence, you know. At times it made me giddy. I hardly knew which was stars and which was phosphorescence, and whether I was swimming on my head or my heels. The canoe was as black as sin, and the ripple under the bows like liquid fire. I was naturally chary of clambering up into it. I was anxious to see what he was up to first. He seemed to be lying cuddled up in a lump in the bows, and the stern was all out of water. The thing kept turning round slowly as it drifted—kind of waltzing, don't you know. I went to the stern, and pulled it down, expecting him to wake up. Then I began to clamber in with my knife in my hand, and ready for a rush. But he never stirred. So there I sat in the stern of the little canoe, drifting away over the calm phosphorescent sea, and with all the host of the stars above me, waiting for something to happen.

"After a long time I called him by name, but he never answered. I was too tired to take any risks by going along to him. So we sat there. I fancy I dozed once or twice. When the dawn came I saw he was as dead as a doornail and all puffed up and purple. My three eggs and the bones were lying in the middle of the canoe, and the keg of water and some coffee and biscuits wrapped in a Cape *Argus* by his feet, and a tin of methylated spirit underneath him. There was no paddle, nor, in fact, anything except the spirit-tin that one could use as one, so I settled to drift until I was picked up. I held an inquest on him, brought in a verdict against some snake, scorpion, or centipede unknown, and sent him overboard.

"After that I had a drink of water and a few biscuits, and took a look round. I suppose a man low down as I was don't see very far; leastways, Madagascar was clean out of sight, and any trace of land at all. I saw a sail going south-westward — looked like a schooner, but her hull never came up. Presently the sun got high in the sky and began to beat down upon me. Lord! It pretty near made my brains boil. I tried dipping my head in the sea, but after a while my eye fell on the Cape *Argus*, and I lay down flat in the canoe and spread this over me. Wonderful things these newspapers! I never read one through thoroughly before, but it's odd what you get up to when you're alone, as I was. I suppose I read that blessed old Cape *Argus* twenty times. The pitch in the canoe simply reeked with the heat and rose up into big blisters.

"I drifted ten days," said the man with the scar. "It's a little thing in the telling, isn't it? Every day was like the last. Except in the morning and the evening I never kept a look-out even — the blaze was so infernal. I didn't see a sail after the first three days, and those I saw took no notice of me. About the sixth night a ship went by scarcely half a mile away from me, with all its lights ablaze and its ports open, looking like a big firefly. There was music aboard. I stood up and shouted and screamed at it. The second day I broached one of the Aepyornis eggs, scraped the shell away at the end bit by bit, and tried it, and I was glad to find it was good enough to eat. A bit flavoury — not bad, I mean — but with something of the taste of a duck's egg. There was a kind of circular patch, about six inches across, on one side of the yolk, and with streaks of blood and a white mark like a ladder in it that I thought queer, but I did not understand what this meant at the time, and I wasn't inclined to be particular. The egg lasted me three days, with biscuits and a drink of water. I chewed coffee berries too — invigorating stuff. The second egg I opened about the eighth day, and it scared me."

The man with the scar paused. "Yes," he said, "developing."

"I dare say you find it hard to believe. *I* did, with the thing before me. There the egg had been, sunk in that cold black mud, perhaps three hundred years. But there was no mistaking it. There was the — what is it? — embryo, with its big head and curved back, and its heart beating under its throat, and the yolk shrivelled up and great membranes spreading inside of the shell and all over the yolk. Here was I hatching out the eggs of the biggest of all extinct birds, in a little canoe in the midst of the Indian Ocean. If old Dawson had known that! It was worth four years' salary. What do *you* think?

"However, I had to eat that precious thing up, every bit of it, before I sighted the reef, and some of the mouthfuls were beastly unpleasant. I left the third one alone. I held it up to the light, but the shell was too thick for me to get any notion of what might be happening inside; and though I fancied I heard blood pulsing, it might have been the rustle in my own ears, like what you listen to in a seashell.

"Then came the atoll. Came out of the sunrise, as it were, suddenly, close up to me. I drifted straight towards it until I was about half a mile from shore, not more, and then the current took a turn, and I had to paddle as hard as I could with my hands and bits of the Aepyornis shell to make the place. However, I got there. It was just a common atoll about four miles round, with a few trees growing and a spring in one place, and the lagoon full of parrot-fish. I took the egg ashore and put it in a good place well above the tide lines and in the sun, to give it all the chance I could, and pulled the canoe up safe, and loafed about prospecting. It's rum how dull an atoll is. As soon as I had found a spring all the interest seemed to vanish. When I was a kid I thought nothing could be finer or more adventurous than the Robinson Crusoe business, but that place was as monotonous as a book of sermons. I went round finding eatable things and generally thinking; but I tell you I was bored to death before the first day was out. It shows my luck—the very day I landed the weather changed. A thunderstorm went by to the north and flicked its wing over the island, and in the night there came a drencher and a howling wind slap over us. It wouldn't have taken much, you know, to upset that canoe.

"I was sleeping under the canoe, and the egg was luckily among the sand higher up the beach, and the first thing I remember was a sound like a hundred pebbles hitting the boat at once, and a rush of water over my body. I'd been dreaming of Antananarivo, and I sat up and holloaed to Intoshi to ask her what the devil was up, and clawed out at the chair where the matches used to be. Then I remembered where I was. There were phosphorescent waves rolling up as if they meant to eat me, and all the rest of the night as black as pitch. The air was simply yelling. The clouds seemed down on your head almost, and the rain fell as if heaven was sinking and they were baling out the waters above the firmament. One great roller came writhing at me, like a fiery serpent, and I bolted. Then I thought of the canoe, and ran down to it as the water went hissing back again; but the thing had gone. I wondered about the egg then, and felt my way to it. It was all right and well out of reach of the maddest waves, so I sat down beside it and cuddled it for company. Lord! what a night that was!

"The storm was over before the morning. There wasn't a rag of cloud left in the sky when the dawn came, and all along the beach there were bits of plank scattered—which was the disarticulated skeleton, so to speak, of my canoe. However, that gave me something to do, for, taking advantage of two of the trees being together, I rigged up a kind of storm-shelter with these vestiges. And that day the egg hatched.

"Hatched, sir, when my head was pillowed on it and I was asleep. I heard a whack and felt a jar and sat up, and there was the end of the egg pecked out and a rum little brown head looking out at me. 'Lord!' I said, 'you're welcome'; and with a little difficulty he came out.

"He was a nice friendly little chap, at first, about the size of a small hen—very much like most other young birds, only bigger. His plumage was a dirty brown to begin with, with a sort of grey scab that fell off it very soon, and scarcely feathers—a kind of downy hair. I can hardly express how pleased I was to see him. I tell you, Robinson Crusoe don't make near enough of his loneliness. But here was interesting company. He looked at me and winked his eye from the front backwards, like a hen, and gave a chirp and began to peck about at once, as though being hatched three hundred years too late was just nothing. 'Glad to see you, Man Friday!' says I, for I had naturally settled he was to be called Man Friday if ever he was hatched, as soon as ever I found the egg in the canoe had developed. I was a bit anxious about his feed, so I gave him a lump of raw parrot-fish at once. He took it, and opened his beak for more. I was glad of that, for, under the circumstances, if he'd been at all fanciful, I should have had to eat him after all. You'd be surprised what an interesting bird that Aepyornis chick was. He followed me about from the very beginning. He used to stand by me and watch while I fished in the lagoon, and go shares in anything I caught. And he was sensible, too. There were nasty green warty things, like pickled gherkins, used to lie about on the beach, and he tried one of these and it upset him. He never even looked at any of them again.

"And he grew. You could almost see him grow. And as I was never much of a society man his quiet, friendly ways suited me to a T. For nearly two years we were as happy as we could be on that island. I had no business worries, for I knew my salary was mounting up at Dawsons'. We would see a sail now and then, but nothing ever came near us. I amused myself, too, by decorating the island with designs worked in sea-urchins and fancy shells of various kinds. I put AEPYORNIS ISLAND all round the place very nearly, in big letters, like what you see done with coloured stones at railway stations in the old country, and mathematical calculations and drawings of various sorts. And I used to lie watching the blessed bird stalking round and growing, growing; and think how I could make a living out of him by showing him about if I ever got taken off. After his first moult he began to get handsome, with a crest and a blue wattle, and a lot of green feathers at the behind of him. And then I used to puzzle whether Dawsons had any right to claim him or not. Stormy weather and in the rainy season we lay snug under the shelter I had made out of the old canoe, and I used to tell him lies about my friends at home. And after a storm we would go round the island together to see if there was any drift. It was a kind of idyll, you might say. If only I had had some tobacco it would have been simply just like Heaven.

"It was about the end of the second year our little paradise went wrong. Friday was then about fourteen feet high to the bill of him, with a big, broad head like the end of a pickaxe, and two huge brown eyes with yellow rims, set together like a man's—not out of sight of each other like a hen's. His plumage was fine—none of the half-mourning style of your ostrich—more like a cassowary as far as colour and texture go. And then it was he began to cock his comb at me and give himself airs, and show signs of a nasty temper....

"At last came a time when my fishing had been rather unlucky, and he began to hang about me in a queer, meditative way. I thought he might have been eating sea-cucumbers or something, but it was really just discontent on his part. I was hungry too, and when at last I landed a fish I wanted it for myself. Tempers were short that morning on both sides. He pecked at it and grabbed it, and I gave him a whack on the head to make him leave go. And at that he went for me. Lord!...

"He gave me this in the face." The man indicated his scar. "Then he kicked me. It was like a cart-horse. I got up, and seeing he hadn't finished, I started off full tilt with my arms doubled up over my face. But he ran on those gawky legs of his faster than a racehorse, and kept landing out at me with sledge hammer kicks, and bringing his pickaxe down on the back of my head. I made for the lagoon, and went in up to my neck. He stopped at the water, for he hated getting his feet wet, and began to make a shindy, something like a peacock's, only hoarser. He started strutting up and down the beach. I'll admit I felt small to see this blessed fossil lording it there. And my head and face were all bleeding, and—well, my body just one jelly of bruises.

"I decided to swim across the lagoon and leave him alone for a bit, until the affair blew over. I shinned up the tallest palm-tree, and sat there thinking of it all. I don't suppose I ever felt so hurt by anything before or since. It was the brutal ingratitude of the creature. I'd been more than a brother to him. I'd hatched him, educated him. A great gawky, out-of-date bird! And me a human being—heir of the ages and all that.

"I thought after a time he'd begin to see things in that light himself, and feel a little sorry for his behaviour. I thought if I was to catch some nice little bits of fish, perhaps, and go to him presently in a casual kind of way, and offer them to him, he might do the sensible thing. It took me some time to learn how unforgiving and cantankerous an extinct bird can be. Malice!

"I won't tell you all the little devices I tried to get that bird round again. I simply can't. It makes my cheek burn with shame even now to think of the snubs and buffets I had from this infernal curiosity. I tried violence. I chucked lumps of coral at him from a safe distance, but he only swallowed them. I shied my open knife at him and almost lost it, though it was too big for him to swallow. I tried starving him out and struck fishing, but he took to picking along the beach at low water after worms, and rubbed along on that. Half my time I spent up to my neck in the lagoon, and the rest up the palm-trees. One of them was scarcely high enough, and when he caught me up it he had a regular Bank Holiday with the calves of my legs. It got unbearable. I don't know if you have ever tried sleeping up a palm-tree. It gave me the most horrible nightmares. Think of the shame of it, too! Here was this extinct animal mooning about my island like a sulky duke, and me not allowed to rest the sole of my foot on the place. I used to cry with weariness and vexation. I told him straight that I didn't mean to be chased about a desert island by any damned anachronisms. I told him to go and peck a navigator of his own age. But he only snapped his beak at me. Great ugly bird—all legs and neck!

"I shouldn't like to say how long that went on altogether. I'd have killed him sooner if I'd known how. However, I hit on a way of settling him at last. It is a South American dodge. I joined all my fishing-lines together with stems of seaweed and things and made a stoutish string, perhaps twelve yards in length or more, and I fastened two lumps of coral rock to the ends of this. It took me some time to do, because every now and then I had to go into the lagoon or up a tree as the fancy took me. This I whirled rapidly round my head, and then let it go at him. The first time I missed, but the next time the string caught his legs beautifully, and wrapped round them again and again. Over he went. I threw it standing waist-deep in the lagoon, and as soon as he went down I was out of the water and sawing at his neck with my knife ...

"I don't like to think of that even now. I felt like a murderer while I did it, though my anger was hot against him. When I stood over him and saw him bleeding on the white sand, and his beautiful great legs and neck writhing in his last agony ... Pah!

"With that tragedy loneliness came upon me like a curse. Good Lord! you can't imagine how I missed that bird. I sat by his corpse and sorrowed over him, and shivered as I looked round the desolate, silent reef. I thought of what a jolly little bird he had been when he was hatched, and of a thousand pleasant tricks he had played before he went wrong. I thought if I'd only wounded him I might have nursed him round into a better understanding. If I'd had any means of digging into the coral rock I'd have buried him. I felt exactly as if he was human. As it was, I couldn't think of eating him, so I put him in the lagoon, and the little fishes picked him clean. I didn't even save the feathers. Then one day a chap cruising about in a yacht had a fancy to see if my atoll still existed.

"He didn't come a moment too soon, for I was about sick enough of the desolation of it, and only hesitating whether I should walk out into the sea and finish up the business that way, or fall back on the green things....

"I sold the bones to a man named Winslow—a dealer near the British Museum, and he says he sold them to old Havers. It seems Havers didn't understand they were extra large, and it was only after his death they attracted attention. They called 'em Aepyornis—what was it?"

"*Aepyornis vastus*," said I. "It's funny, the very thing was mentioned to me by a friend of mine. When they found an Aepyornis, with a thigh a yard long, they thought they had reached the top of the scale, and called him *Aepyornis maximus*. Then someone turned up another thighbone four feet six or more, and that they called *Aepyornis Titan*. Then your *vastus* was found after old Havers died, in his collection, and then a *vastissimus* turned up."

"Winslow was telling me as much," said the man with the scar. "If they get any more Aepyornises, he reckons some scientific swell will go and burst a blood-vessel. But it was a queer thing to happen to a man; wasn't it—altogether?"

THE REMARKABLE CASE OF DAVIDSON'S EYES

The transitory mental aberration of Sidney Davidson, remarkable enough in itself, is still more remarkable if Wade's explanation is to be credited. It sets one dreaming of the oddest possibilities of intercommunication in the future, of spending an intercalary five minutes on the other side of the world, or being watched in our most secret operations by unsuspected eyes. It happened that I was the immediate witness of Davidson's seizure, and so it falls naturally to me to put the story upon paper.

When I say that I was the immediate witness of his seizure, I mean that I was the first on the scene. The thing happened at the Harlow Technical College, just beyond the Highgate Archway. He was alone in the larger laboratory when the thing happened. I was in a smaller room, where the balances are, writing up some notes. The thunderstorm had completely upset my work, of course. It was just after one of the louder peals that I thought I heard some glass smash in the other room. I stopped writing, and turned round to listen. For a moment I heard nothing; the hail was playing the devil's tattoo on the corrugated zinc of the roof. Then came another sound, a smash—no doubt of it this time. Something heavy had been knocked off the bench. I jumped up at once and went and opened the door leading into the big laboratory.

I was surprised to hear a queer sort of laugh, and saw Davidson standing unsteadily in the middle of the room, with a dazzled look on his face. My first impression was that he was drunk. He did not notice me. He was clawing out at something invisible a yard in front of his face. He put out his hand, slowly, rather hesitatingly, and then clutched nothing. "What's come to it?" he said. He held up his hands to his face, fingers spread out. "Great Scot!" he said. The thing happened three or four years ago, when everyone swore by that personage. Then he began raising his feet clumsily, as though he had expected to find them glued to the floor.

"Davidson!" cried I. "What's the matter with you?" He turned round in my direction and looked about for me. He looked over me and at me and on either side of me, without the slightest sign of seeing me. "Waves," he said; "and a remarkably neat schooner. I'd swear that was Bellows' voice. *Hullo*!" He shouted suddenly at the top of his voice.

I thought he was up to some foolery. Then I saw littered about his feet the shattered remains of the best of our electrometers. "What's up, man?" said I. "You've smashed the electrometer!"

"Bellows again!" said he. "Friends left, if my hands are gone. Something about electrometers. Which way *are* you, Bellows?" He suddenly came staggering towards me. "The damned stuff cuts like butter," he said. He walked straight into the bench and recoiled. "None so buttery that!" he said, and stood swaying.

I felt scared. "Davidson," said I, "what on earth's come over you?"

He looked round him in every direction. "I could swear that was Bellows. Why don't you show yourself like a man, Bellows?"

It occurred to me that he must be suddenly struck blind. I walked round the table and laid my hand upon his arm. I never saw a man more startled in my life. He jumped away from me, and came round into an attitude of self-defence, his face fairly distorted with terror. "Good God!" he cried. "What was that?"

"It's I—Bellows. Confound it, Davidson!"

He jumped when I answered him and stared—how can I express it?—right through me. He began talking, not to me, but to himself. "Here in broad daylight on a clear beach. Not a place to hide in." He looked about him wildly. "Here! I'm *off*." He suddenly turned and ran headlong into the big electro-magnet—so violently that, as we found afterwards, he bruised his shoulder and jawbone cruelly. At that he stepped back a pace, and cried out with almost a whimper, "What, in heaven's name, has come over me?" He stood, blanched with terror and trembling violently, with his right arm clutching his left, where that had collided with the magnet.

By that time I was excited and fairly scared. "Davidson," said I, "don't be afraid."

He was startled at my voice, but not so excessively as before. I repeated my words in as clear and firm a tone as I could assume. "Bellows," he said, "is that you?"

"Can't you see it's me?"

He laughed. "I can't even see it's myself. Where the devil are we?"

"Here," said I, "in the laboratory."

"The laboratory!" he answered, in a puzzled tone, and put his hand to his forehead. "I *was* in the laboratory—till that flash came, but I'm hanged if I'm there now. What ship is that?"

"There's no ship," said I. "Do be sensible, old chap."

"No ship!" he repeated, and seemed to forget my denial forthwith. "I suppose," said he, slowly, "we're both dead. But the rummy part is I feel just as though I still had a body. Don't get used to it all at once, I suppose. The old shop was struck by lightning, I suppose. Jolly quick thing, Bellows—eigh?"

"Don't talk nonsense. You're very much alive. You are in the laboratory, blundering about. You've just smashed a new electrometer. I don't envy you when Boyce arrives."

He stared away from me towards the diagrams of cryohydrates. "I must be deaf," said he. "They've fired a gun, for there goes the puff of smoke, and I never heard a sound."

I put my hand on his arm again, and this time he was less alarmed. "We seem to have a sort of invisible bodies," said he. "By Jove! there's a boat coming round the headland. It's very much like the old life after all—in a different climate."

I shook his arm. "Davidson," I cried, "wake up!"

II.

It was just then that Boyce came in. So soon as he spoke Davidson exclaimed: "Old Boyce! Dead too! What a lark!" I hastened to explain that Davidson was in a kind of somnambulistic trance. Boyce was interested at once. We both did all we could to rouse the fellow out of his extraordinary state. He answered our questions, and asked us some of his own, but his attention seemed distracted by his hallucination about a beach and a ship. He kept interpolating observations concerning some boat and the davits and sails filling with the wind. It made one feel queer, in the dusky laboratory, to hear him saying such things.

He was blind and helpless. We had to walk him down the passage, one at each elbow, to Boyce's private room, and while Boyce talked to him there, and humoured him about this ship idea, I went along the corridor and asked old Wade to come and look at him. The voice of our Dean sobered him a little, but not very much. He asked where his hands were, and why he had to walk about up to his waist in the ground. Wade thought over him a long time—you know how he knits his brows—and then made him feel the couch, guiding his hands to it. "That's a couch," said Wade. "The couch in the private room of Professor Boyce. Horsehair stuffing."

Davidson felt about, and puzzled over it, and answered presently that he could feel it all right, but he couldn't see it.

"What *do* you see?" asked Wade. Davidson said he could see nothing but a lot of sand and broken-up shells. Wade gave him some other things to feel, telling him what they were, and watching him keenly.

"The ship is almost hull down," said Davidson, presently, *apropos* of nothing.

"Never mind the ship," said Wade. "Listen to me, Davidson. Do you know what hallucination means?"

"Rather," said Davidson.

"Well, everything you see is hallucinatory."

"Bishop Berkeley," said Davidson.

"Don't mistake me," said Wade. "You are alive and in this room of Boyce's. But something has happened to your eyes. You cannot see; you can feel and hear, but not see. Do you follow me?"

"It seems to me that I see too much." Davidson rubbed his knuckles into his eyes. "Well?" he said.

"That's all. Don't let it perplex you. Bellows, here, and I will take you home in a cab."

"Wait a bit." Davidson thought. "Help me to sit down," said he, presently; "and now—I'm sorry to trouble you—but will you tell me all that over again?"

Wade repeated it very patiently. Davidson shut his eyes, and pressed his hands upon his forehead. "Yes," said he. "It's quite right. Now my eyes are shut I know you're right. That's you, Bellows, sitting by me on the couch. I'm in England again. And we're in the dark."

Then he opened his eyes, "And there," said he, "is the sun just rising, and the yards of the ship, and a tumbled sea, and a couple of birds flying. I never saw anything so real. And I'm sitting up to my neck in a bank of sand."

He bent forward and covered his face with his hands. Then he opened his eyes again. "Dark sea and sunrise! And yet I'm sitting on a sofa in old Boyce's room! ... God help me!"

III.

That was the beginning. For three weeks this strange affection of Davidson's eyes continued unabated. It was far worse than being blind. He was absolutely helpless, and had to be fed like a newly-hatched bird, and led about and undressed. If he attempted to move he fell over things or stuck himself against walls or doors. After a day or so he got used to hearing our voices without seeing us, and willingly admitted he was at home, and that Wade was right in what he told him. My sister, to whom he was engaged, insisted on coming to see him, and would sit for hours every day while he talked about this beach of his. Holding her hand seemed to comfort him immensely. He explained that when we left the College and drove home—he lived in Hampstead village—it appeared to him as if we drove right through a sandhill—it was perfectly black until he emerged again—and through rocks and trees and solid obstacles, and when he was taken to his own room it made him giddy and almost frantic with the fear of falling, because going upstairs seemed to lift him thirty or forty feet above the rocks of his imaginary island. He kept saying he should smash all the eggs. The end was that he had to be taken down into his father's consulting room and laid upon a couch that stood there.

He described the island as being a bleak kind of place on the whole, with very little vegetation, except some peaty stuff, and a lot of bare rock. There were multitudes of penguins, and they made the rocks white and disagreeable to see. The sea was often rough, and once there was a thunderstorm, and he lay and shouted at the silent flashes. Once or twice seals pulled up on the beach, but only on the first two or three days. He said it was very funny the way in which the penguins used to waddle right through him, and how he seemed to lie among them without disturbing them.

I remember one odd thing, and that was when he wanted very badly to smoke. We put a pipe in his hands—he almost poked his eye out with it—and lit it. But he couldn't taste anything. I've since found it's the same with me—I don't know if it's the usual case—that I cannot enjoy tobacco at all unless I can see the smoke.

But the queerest part of his vision came when Wade sent him out in a bath-chair to get fresh air. The Davidsons hired a chair, and got that deaf and obstinate dependent of theirs, Widgery, to attend to it. Widgery's ideas of healthy expeditions were peculiar. My sister, who had been to the Dogs' Home, met them in Camden Town, towards King's Cross, Widgery trotting along complacently, and Davidson evidently most distressed, trying in his feeble, blind way to attract Widgery's attention.

He positively wept when my sister spoke to him. "Oh, get me out of this horrible darkness!" he said, feeling for her hand. "I must get out of it, or I shall die." He was quite incapable of explaining what was the matter, but my sister decided he must go home, and presently, as they went up hill towards Hampstead, the horror seemed to drop from him. He said it was good to see the stars again, though it was then about noon and a blazing day.

"It seemed," he told me afterwards, "as if I was being carried irresistibly towards the water. I was not very much alarmed at first. Of course it was night there—a lovely night."

"Of course?" I asked, for that struck me as odd.

"Of course," said he. "It's always night there when it is day here…. Well, we went right into the water, which was calm and shining under the moonlight—just a broad swell that seemed to grow broader and flatter as I came down into it. The surface glistened just like a skin—it might have been empty space underneath for all I could tell to the contrary. Very slowly, for I rode slanting into it, the water crept up to my eyes. Then I went under and the skin seemed to break and heal again about my eyes. The moon gave a jump up in the sky and grew green and dim, and fish, faintly glowing, came darting round me—and things that seemed made of luminous glass, and I passed through a tangle of seaweeds that shone with an oily lustre. And so I drove down into the sea, and the stars went out one by one, and the moon grew greener and darker, and the seaweed became a luminous purple-red. It was all very faint and mysterious, and everything seemed to quiver. And all the while I could hear the wheels of the bath-chair creaking, and the footsteps of people going by, and a man in the distance selling the special *Pall Mall.*

"I kept sinking down deeper and deeper into the water. It became inky black about me, not a ray from above came down into that darkness, and the phosphorescent things grew brighter and brighter. The snaky branches of the deeper weeds flickered like the flames of spirit lamps; but, after a time, there were no more weeds. The fishes came staring and gaping towards me, and into me and through me. I never imagined such fishes before. They had lines of fire along the sides of them as though they had been outlined with a luminous pencil. And there was a ghastly thing swimming backwards with a lot of twining arms. And then I saw, coming very slowly towards me through the gloom, a hazy mass of light that resolved itself as it drew nearer into multitudes of fishes, struggling and darting round something that drifted. I drove on straight towards it, and presently I saw in the midst of the tumult, and by the light of the fish, a bit of splintered spar looming over me, and a dark hull tilting over, and some glowing phosphorescent forms that were shaken and writhed as the fish bit at them. Then it was I began to try to attract Widgery's attention. A horror came upon me. Ugh! I should have driven right into those half-eaten—things. If your sister had not come! They had great holes in them, Bellows, and … Never mind. But it was ghastly!"

IV.

For three weeks Davidson remained in this singular state, seeing what at the time we imagined was an altogether phantasmal world, and stone blind to the world around him. Then, one Tuesday, when I called I met old Davidson in the passage. "He can see his thumb!" the old gentleman said, in a perfect transport. He was struggling into his overcoat. "He can see his thumb, Bellows!" he said, with the tears in his eyes. "The lad will be all right yet."

I rushed in to Davidson. He was holding up a little book before his face, and looking at it and laughing in a weak kind of way.

"It's amazing," said he. "There's a kind of patch come there." He pointed with his finger. "I'm on the rocks as usual, and the penguins are staggering and flapping about as usual, and there's been a whale showing every now and then, but it's got too dark now to make him out. But put something *there,* and I see it—I do see it. It's very dim and broken in places, but I see it all the same, like a faint spectre of itself. I found it out this morning while they were dressing me. It's like a hole in this infernal phantom world. Just put your hand by mine. No—not there. Ah! Yes! I see it. The base of your thumb and a bit of cuff! It looks like the ghost of a bit of your hand sticking out of the darkling sky. Just by it there's a group of stars like a cross coming out."

From that time Davidson began to mend. His account of the change, like his account of the vision, was oddly convincing. Over patches of his field of vision, the phantom world grew fainter, grew transparent, as it were, and through these translucent gaps he began to see dimly the real world about him. The patches grew in size and number, ran together and spread until only here and there were blind spots left upon his eyes. He was able to get up and steer himself about, feed himself once more, read, smoke, and behave like an ordinary citizen again. At first it was very confusing to him to have these two pictures overlapping each other like the changing views of a lantern, but in a little while he began to distinguish the real from the illusory.

At first he was unfeignedly glad, and seemed only too anxious to complete his cure by taking exercise and tonics. But as that odd island of his began to fade away from him, he became queerly interested in it. He wanted particularly to go down into the deep sea again, and would spend half his time wandering about the low lying parts of London, trying to find the water-logged wreck he had seen drifting. The glare of real daylight very soon impressed him so vividly as to blot out everything of his shadowy world, but of a night time, in a darkened room, he could still see the white-splashed rocks of the island, and the clumsy penguins staggering to and fro. But even these grew fainter and fainter, and, at last, soon after he married my sister, he saw them for the last time.

V.

And now to tell of the queerest thing of all. About two years after his cure I dined with the Davidsons, and after dinner a man named Atkins called in. He is a lieutenant in the Royal Navy, and a pleasant, talkative man. He was on friendly terms with my brother-in-law, and was soon on friendly terms with me. It came out that he was engaged to Davidson's cousin, and incidentally he took out a kind of pocket photograph case to show us a new rendering of *fiancée*. "And, by-the-by," said he, "here's the old *Fulmar*."

Davidson looked at it casually. Then suddenly his face lit up. "Good heavens!" said he. "I could almost swear—"

"What?" said Atkins.

"That I had seen that ship before."

"Don't see how you can have. She hasn't been out of the South Seas for six years, and before then—"

"But," began Davidson, and then, "Yes—that's the ship I dreamt of, I'm sure that's the ship I dreamt of. She was standing off an island that swarmed with penguins, and she fired a gun."

"Good Lord!" said Atkins, who had now heard the particulars of the seizure. "How the deuce could you dream that?"

And then, bit by bit, it came out that on the very day Davidson was seized, H.M.S. *Fulmar* had actually been off a little rock to the south of Antipodes Island. A boat had landed overnight to get penguins' eggs, had been delayed, and a thunderstorm drifting up, the boat's crew had waited until the morning before rejoining the ship. Atkins had been one of them, and he corroborated, word for word, the descriptions Davidson had given of the island and the boat. There is not the slightest doubt in any of our minds that Davidson has really seen the place. In some unaccountable way, while he moved hither and thither in London, his sight moved hither and thither in a manner that corresponded, about this distant island. *How* is absolutely a mystery.

That completes the remarkable story of Davidson's eyes. It's perhaps the best authenticated case in existence of a real vision at a distance. Explanation there is none forthcoming, except what Professor Wade has thrown out. But his explanation invokes the Fourth Dimension, and a dissertation on theoretical kinds of space. To talk of there being "a kink in space" seems mere nonsense to me; it may be because I am no mathematician. When I said that nothing would alter the fact that the place is eight thousand miles away, he answered that two points might be a yard away on a sheet of paper and yet be brought together by bending the paper round. The reader may grasp his argument, but I certainly do not. His idea seems to be that Davidson, stooping between the poles of the big electro-magnet, had some extraordinary twist given to his retinal elements through the sudden change in the field of force due to the lightning.

He thinks, as a consequence of this, that it may be possible to live visually in one part of the world, while one lives bodily in another. He has even made some experiments in support of his views; but, so far, he has simply succeeded in blinding a few dogs. I believe that is the net result of his work, though I have not seen him for some weeks. Latterly I have been so busy with my work in connection with the Saint Pancras installation that I have had little opportunity of calling to see him. But the whole of his theory seems fantastic to me. The facts concerning Davidson stand on an altogether different footing, and I can testify personally to the accuracy of every detail I have given.

THE LORD OF THE DYNAMOS

The chief attendant of the three dynamos that buzzed and rattled at Camberwell, and kept the electric railway going, came out of Yorkshire, and his name was James Holroyd. He was a practical electrician, but fond of whisky, a heavy, red-haired brute with irregular teeth. He doubted the existence of the deity, but accepted Carnot's cycle, and he had read Shakespeare and found him weak in chemistry. His helper came out of the mysterious East, and his name was Azuma-zi. But Holroyd called him Pooh-bah. Holroyd liked a nigger help because he would stand kicking—a habit with Holroyd—and did not pry into the machinery and try to learn the ways of it. Certain odd possibilities of the negro mind brought into abrupt contact with the crown of our civilisation Holroyd never fully realised, though just at the end he got some inkling of them.

To define Azuma-zi was beyond ethnology. He was, perhaps, more negroid than anything else, though his hair was curly rather than frizzy, and his nose had a bridge. Moreover, his skin was brown rather than black, and the whites of his eyes were yellow. His broad cheek-bones and narrow chin gave his face something of the viperine V. His head, too, was broad behind, and low and narrow at the forehead, as if his brain had been twisted round in the reverse way to a European's. He was short of stature and still shorter of English. In conversation he made numerous odd noises of no known marketable value, and his infrequent words were carved and wrought into heraldic grotesqueness. Holroyd tried to elucidate his religious beliefs, and—especially after whiskey—lectured to him against superstition and missionaries. Azuma-zi, however, shirked the discussion of his gods, even though he was kicked for it.

Azuma-zi had come, clad in white but insufficient raiment, out of the stokehole of the *Lord Clive*, from the Straits Settlements, and beyond, into London. He had heard even in his youth of the greatness and riches of London, where all the women are white and fair, and even the beggars in the streets are white, and he had arrived, with newly-earned gold coins in his pocket, to worship at the shrine of civilisation. The day of his landing was a dismal one; the sky was dun, and a wind-worried drizzle filtered down to the greasy streets, but he plunged boldly into the delights of Shadwell, and was presently cast up, shattered in health, civilised in costume, penniless, and, except in matters of the direst necessity, practically a dumb animal, to toil for James Holroyd and to be bullied by him in the dynamo shed at Camberwell. And to James Holroyd bullying was a labour of love.

There were three dynamos with their engines at Camberwell. The two that have been there since the beginning are small machines; the larger one was new.

The smaller machines made a reasonable noise; their straps hummed over the drums, every now and then the brushes buzzed and fizzled, and the air churned steadily, whoo! whoo! whoo! between their poles. One was loose in its foundations and kept the shed vibrating. But the big dynamo drowned these little noises altogether with the sustained drone of its iron core, which somehow set part of the ironwork humming. The place made the visitor's head reel with the throb, throb, throb of the engines, the rotation of the big wheels, the spinning ball-valves, the occasional spittings of the steam, and over all the deep, unceasing, surging note of the big dynamo. This last noise was from an engineering point of view a defect, but Azuma-zi accounted it unto the monster for mightiness and pride.

If it were possible we would have the noises of that shed always about the reader as he reads, we would tell all our story to such an accompaniment. It was a steady stream of din, from which the ear picked out first one thread and then another; there was the intermittent snorting, panting, and seething of the steam engines, the suck and thud of their pistons, the dull beat on the air as the spokes of the great driving-wheels came round, a note the leather straps made as they ran tighter and looser, and a fretful tumult from the dynamos; and over all, sometimes inaudible, as the ear tired of it, and then creeping back upon the senses again, was this trombone note of the big machine. The floor never felt steady and quiet beneath one's feet, but quivered and jarred. It was a confusing, unsteady place, and enough to send anyone's thoughts jerking into odd zigzags. And for three months, while the big strike of the engineers was in progress, Holroyd, who was a blackleg, and Azuma-zi, who was a mere black, were never out of the stir and eddy of it, but slept and fed in the little wooden shanty between the shed and the gates.

Holroyd delivered a theological lecture on the text of his big machine soon after Azuma-zi came. He had to shout to be heard in the din. "Look at that," said Holroyd; "where's your 'eathen idol to match 'im?" And Azuma-zi looked. For a moment Holroyd was inaudible, and then Azuma-zi heard: "Kill a hundred men. Twelve per cent, on the ordinary shares," said Holroyd, "and that's something like a Gord!"

Holroyd was proud of his big dynamo, and expatiated upon its size and power to Azuma-zi until heaven knows what odd currents of thought that and the incessant whirling and shindy set up within the curly black cranium. He would explain in the most graphic manner the dozen or so ways in which a man might be killed by it, and once he gave Azuma-zi a shock as a sample of its quality. After that, in the breathing-times of his labour—it was heavy labour, being not only his own, but most of Holroyd's—Azuma-zi would sit and watch the big machine. Now and then the brushes would sparkle and spit blue flashes, at which Holroyd would swear, but all the rest was as smooth and rhythmic as breathing. The band ran shouting over the shaft, and ever behind one as one watched was the complacent thud of the piston. So it lived all day in this big airy shed, with him and Holroyd to wait upon it; not prisoned up and slaving to drive a ship as the other engines he knew—mere captive devils of the British Solomon—had been, but a machine enthroned. Those two smaller dynamos, Azuma-zi by force of contrast despised; the large one he privately christened the Lord of the Dynamos. They were fretful and irregular, but the big dynamo was steady. How great it was! How serene and easy in its working! Greater and calmer even than the Buddahs he had seen at Rangoon, and yet not motionless, but living! The great black coils spun, spun, spun, the rings ran round under the brushes, and the deep note of its coil steadied the whole. It affected Azuma-zi queerly.

Azuma-zi was not fond of labour. He would sit about and watch the Lord of the Dynamos while Holroyd went away to persuade the yard porter to get whiskey, although his proper place was not in the dynamo shed but behind the engines, and, moreover, if Holroyd caught him skulking he got hit for it with a rod of stout copper wire. He would go and stand close to the colossus and look up at the great leather band running overhead. There was a black patch on the band that came round, and it pleased him somehow among all the clatter to watch this return again and again. Odd thoughts spun with the whirl of it. Scientific people tell us that savages give souls to rocks and trees—and a machine is a thousand times more alive than a rock or a tree. And Azuma-zi was practically a savage still; the veneer of civilisation lay no deeper than his slop suit, his bruises, and the coal grime on his face and hands. His father before him had worshipped a meteoric stone, kindred blood it may be had splashed the broad wheels of Juggernaut.

He took every opportunity Holroyd gave him of touching and handling the great dynamo that was fascinating him. He polished and cleaned it until the metal parts were blinding in the sun. He felt a mysterious sense of service in doing this. He would go up to it and touch its spinning coils gently. The gods he had worshipped were all far away. The people in London hid their gods.

At last his dim feelings grew more distinct, and took shape in thoughts and at last in acts. When he came into the roaring shed one morning he salaamed to the Lord of the Dynamos, and then, when Holroyd was away, he went and whispered to the thundering machine that he was its servant, and prayed it to have pity on him and save him from Holroyd. As he did so a rare gleam of light came in through the open archway of the throbbing machine-shed, and the Lord of the Dynamos, as he whirled and roared, was radiant with pale gold. Then Azuma-zi knew that his service was acceptable to his Lord. After that he did not feel so lonely as he had done, and he had indeed been very much alone in London. And even when his work time was over, which was rare, he loitered about the shed.

Then, the next time Holroyd maltreated him, Azuma-zi went presently to the Lord of the Dynamos and whispered, "Thou seest, O my Lord!" and the angry whirr of the machinery seemed to answer him. Thereafter it appeared to him that whenever Holroyd came into the shed a different note came into the sounds of the dynamo. "My Lord bides his time," said Azuma-zi to himself. "The iniquity of the fool is not yet ripe." And he waited and watched for the day of reckoning. One day there was evidence of short circuiting, and Holroyd, making an unwary examination—it was in the afternoon—got a rather severe shock. Azuma-zi from behind the engine saw him jump off and curse at the peccant coil.

"He is warned," said Azuma-zi to himself. "Surely my Lord is very patient."

Holroyd had at first initiated his "nigger" into such elementary conceptions of the dynamo's working as would enable him to take temporary charge of the shed in his absence. But when he noticed the manner in which Azuma-zi hung about the monster he became suspicious. He dimly perceived his assistant was "up to something," and connecting him with the anointing of the coils with oil that had rotted the varnish in one place, he issued an edict, shouted above the confusion of the machinery, "Don't 'ee go nigh that big dynamo any more, Pooh-bah, or a'll take thy skin off!" Besides, if it pleased Azuma-zi to be near the big machine, it was plain sense and decency to keep him away from it.

Azuma-zi obeyed at the time, but later he was caught bowing before the Lord of the Dynamos. At which Holroyd twisted his arm and kicked him as he turned to go away. As Azuma-zi presently stood behind the engine and glared at the back of the hated Holroyd, the noises of the machinery took a new rhythm, and sounded like four words in his native tongue.

It is hard to say exactly what madness is. I fancy Azuma-zi was mad. The incessant din and whirl of the dynamo shed may have churned up his little store of knowledge and big store of superstitious fancy, at last, into something akin to frenzy. At any rate, when the idea of making Holroyd a sacrifice to the Dynamo Fetich was thus suggested to him, it filled him with a strange tumult of exultant emotion.

That night the two men and their black shadows were alone in the shed together. The shed was lit with one big arc light that winked and flickered purple. The shadows lay black behind the dynamos, the ball governors of the engines whirled from light to darkness, and their pistons beat loud and steady. The world outside seen through the open end of the shed seemed incredibly dim and remote. It seemed absolutely silent, too, since the riot of the machinery drowned every external sound. Far away was the black fence of the yard with grey shadowy houses behind, and above was the deep blue sky and the pale little stars. Azuma-zi suddenly walked across the centre of the shed above which the leather bands were running, and went into the shadow by the big dynamo. Holroyd heard a click, and the spin of the armature changed.

"What are you dewin' with that switch?" he bawled in surprise. "Han't I told you—"

Then he saw the set expression of Azuma-zi's eyes as the Asiatic came out of the shadow towards him.

In another moment the two men were grappling fiercely in front of the great dynamo.

"You coffee-headed fool!" gasped Holroyd, with a brown hand at his throat. "Keep off those contact rings." In another moment he was tripped and reeling back upon the Lord of the Dynamos. He instinctively loosened his grip upon his antagonist to save himself from the machine.

The messenger, sent in furious haste from the station to find out what had happened in the dynamo shed, met Azuma-zi at the porter's lodge by the gate. Azuma-zi tried to explain something, but the messenger could make nothing of the black's incoherent English, and hurried on to the shed. The machines were all noisily at work, and nothing seemed to be disarranged. There was, however, a queer smell of singed hair. Then he saw an odd-looking crumpled mass clinging to the front of the big dynamo, and, approaching, recognised the distorted remains of Holroyd.

The man stared and hesitated a moment. Then he saw the face, and shut his eyes convulsively. He turned on his heel before he opened them, so that he should not see Holroyd again, and went out of the shed to get advice and help.

When Azuma-zi saw Holroyd die in the grip of the Great Dynamo he had been a little scared about the consequences of his act. Yet he felt strangely elated, and knew that the favour of the Lord Dynamo was upon him. His plan was already settled when he met the man coming from the station, and the scientific manager who speedily arrived on the scene jumped at the obvious conclusion of suicide. This expert scarcely noticed Azuma-zi, except to ask a few questions. Did he see Holroyd kill himself? Azuma-zi explained he had been out of sight at the engine furnace until he heard a difference in the noise from the dynamo. It was not a difficult examination, being untinctured by suspicion.

The distorted remains of Holroyd, which the electrician removed from the machine, were hastily covered by the porter with a coffee-stained tablecloth. Somebody, by a happy inspiration, fetched a medical man. The expert was chiefly anxious to get the machine at work again, for seven or eight trains had stopped midway in the stuffy tunnels of the electric railway. Azuma-zi, answering or misunderstanding the questions of the people who had by authority or impudence come into the shed, was presently sent back to the stoke-hole by the scientific manager. Of course a crowd collected outside the gates of the yard—a crowd, for no known reason, always hovers for a day or two near the scene of a sudden death in London—two or three reporters percolated somehow into the engine-shed, and one even got to Azuma-zi; but the scientific expert cleared them out again, being himself an amateur journalist.

Presently the body was carried away, and public interest departed with it. Azuma-zi remained very quietly at his furnace, seeing over and over again in the coals a figure that wriggled violently and became still. An hour after the murder, to anyone coming into the shed it would have looked exactly as if nothing remarkable had ever happened there. Peeping presently from his engine-room the black saw the Lord Dynamo spin and whirl beside his little brothers, and the driving wheels were beating round, and the steam in the pistons went thud, thud, exactly as it had been earlier in the evening. After all, from the mechanical point of view, it had been a most insignificant incident—the mere temporary deflection of a current. But now the slender form and slender shadow of the scientific manager replaced the sturdy outline of Holroyd travelling up and down the lane of light upon the vibrating floor under the straps between the engines and the dynamos.

"Have I not served my Lord?" said Azuma-zi inaudibly, from his shadow, and the note of the great dynamo rang out full and clear. As he looked at the big whirling mechanism the strange fascination of it that had been a little in abeyance since Holroyd's death resumed its sway.

Never had Azuma-zi seen a man killed so swiftly and pitilessly. The big humming machine had slain its victim without wavering for a second from its steady beating. It was indeed a mighty god.

The unconscious scientific manager stood with his back to him, scribbling on a piece of paper. His shadow lay at the foot of the monster.

"Was the Lord Dynamo still hungry? His servant was ready."

Azuma-zi made a stealthy step forward; then stopped. The scientific manager suddenly stopped writing, and walked down the shed to the endmost of the dynamos, and began to examine the brushes.

Azuma-zi hesitated, and then slipped across noiselessly into the shadow by the switch. There he waited. Presently the manager's footsteps could be heard returning. He stopped in his old position, unconscious of the stoker crouching ten feet away from him. Then the big dynamo suddenly fizzled, and in another moment Azuma-zi had sprung out of the darkness upon him.

First, the scientific manager was gripped round the body and swung towards the big dynamo, then, kicking with his knee and forcing his antagonist's head down with his hands, he loosened the grip on his waist and swung round away from the machine. Then the black grasped him again, putting a curly head against his chest, and they swayed and panted as it seemed for an age or so. Then the scientific manager was impelled to catch a black ear in his teeth and bite furiously. The black yelled hideously.

They rolled over on the floor, and the black, who had apparently slipped from the vice of the teeth or parted with some ear—the scientific manager wondered which at the time—tried to throttle him. The scientific manager was making some ineffectual efforts to claw something with his hands and to kick, when the welcome sound of quick footsteps sounded on the floor. The next moment Azuma-zi had left him and darted towards the big dynamo. There was a splutter amid the roar.

The officer of the company who had entered, stood staring as Azuma-zi caught the naked terminals in his hands, gave one horrible convulsion, and then hung motionless from the machine, his face violently distorted.

"I'm jolly glad you came in when you did," said the scientific manager, still sitting on the floor.

He looked at the still quivering figure. "It is not a nice death to die, apparently—but it is quick."

The official was still staring at the body. He was a man of slow apprehension.

There was a pause.

The scientific manager got up on his feet rather awkwardly. He ran his fingers along his collar thoughtfully, and moved his head to and fro several times.

"Poor Holroyd! I see now." Then almost mechanically he went towards the switch in the shadow and turned the current into the railway circuit again. As he did so the singed body loosened its grip upon the machine and fell forward on its face. The core of the dynamo roared out loud and clear, and the armature beat the air.

So ended prematurely the Worship of the Dynamo Deity, perhaps the most short-lived of all religions. Yet withal it could at least boast a Martyrdom and a Human Sacrifice.

THE HAMMERPOND PARK BURGLARY

It is a moot point whether burglary is to be considered as a sport, a trade, or an art. For a trade, the technique is scarcely rigid enough, and its claims to be considered an art are vitiated by the mercenary element that qualifies its triumphs. On the whole it seems to be most justly ranked as sport, a sport for which no rules are at present formulated, and of which the prizes are distributed in an extremely informal manner. It was this informality of burglary that led to the regrettable extinction of two promising beginners at Hammerpond Park.

The stakes offered in this affair consisted chiefly of diamonds and other personal *bric-à-brac* belonging to the newly married Lady Aveling. Lady Aveling, as the reader will remember, was the only daughter of Mrs Montague Pangs, the well-known hostess. Her marriage to Lord Aveling was extensively advertised in the papers, the quantity and quality of her wedding presents, and the fact that the honeymoon was to be spent at Hammerpond. The announcement of these valuable prizes created a considerable sensation in the small circle in which Mr Teddy Watkins was the undisputed leader, and it was decided that, accompanied by a duly qualified assistant, he should visit the village of Hammerpond in his professional capacity.

Being a man of naturally retiring and modest disposition, Mr Watkins determined to make this visit *incog.*, and after due consideration of the conditions of his enterprise, he selected the rôle of a landscape artist and the unassuming surname of Smith. He preceded his assistant, who, it was decided, should join him only on the last afternoon of his stay at Hammerpond. Now the village of Hammerpond is perhaps one of the prettiest little corners in Sussex; many thatched houses still survive, the flint-built church with its tall spire nestling under the down is one of the finest and least restored in the county, and the beech-woods and bracken jungles through which the road runs to the great house are singularly rich in what the vulgar artist and photographer call "bits." So that Mr Watkins, on his arrival with two virgin canvases, a brand-new easel, a paint-box, portmanteau, an ingenious little ladder made in sections (after the pattern of the late lamented master Charles Peace), crowbar, and wire coils, found himself welcomed with effusion and some curiosity by half-a-dozen other brethren of the brush. It rendered the disguise he had chosen unexpectedly plausible, but it inflicted upon him a considerable amount of aesthetic conversation for which he was very imperfectly prepared.

"Have you exhibited very much?" said Young Porson in the bar-parlour of the "Coach and Horses," where Mr Watkins was skilfully accumulating local information on the night of his arrival.

"Very little," said Mr Watkins, "just a snack here and there."

"Academy?"

"In course. *And* the Crystal Palace."

"Did they hang you well?" said Porson.

"Don't rot," said Mr Watkins; "I don't like it."

"I mean did they put you in a good place?"

"Whadyer mean?" said Mr Watkins suspiciously. "One 'ud think you were trying to make out I'd been put away."

Porson had been brought up by aunts, and was a gentlemanly young man even for an artist; he did not know what being "put away" meant, but he thought it best to explain that he intended nothing of the sort. As the question of hanging seemed a sore point with Mr Watkins, he tried to divert the conversation a little.

"Do you do figure-work at all?"

"No, never had a head for figures," said Mr Watkins, "my miss—Mrs Smith, I mean, does all that."

"She paints too!" said Porson. "That's rather jolly."

"Very," said Mr Watkins, though he really did not think so, and, feeling the conversation was drifting a little beyond his grasp, added, "I came down here to paint Hammerpond House by moonlight."

"Really!" said Porson. "That's rather a novel idea."

"Yes," said Mr Watkins, "I thought it rather a good notion when it occurred to me. I expect to begin to-morrow night."

"What! You don't mean to paint in the open, by night?"

"I do, though."

"But how will you see your canvas?"

"Have a bloomin' cop's—" began Mr Watkins, rising too quickly to the question, and then realising this, bawled to Miss Durgan for another glass of beer. "I'm goin' to have a thing called a dark lantern," he said to Porson.

"But it's about new moon now," objected Porson. "There won't be any moon."

"There'll be the house," said Watkins, "at any rate. I'm goin', you see, to paint the house first and the moon afterwards."

"Oh!" said Porson, too staggered to continue the conversation.

"They doo say," said old Durgan, the landlord, who had maintained a respectful silence during the technical conversation, "as there's no less than three p'licemen from 'Azelworth on dewty every night in the house—'count of this Lady Aveling 'n her jewellery. One'm won fower-and-six last night, off second footman—tossin'."

Towards sunset next day Mr Watkins, virgin canvas, easel, and a very considerable case of other appliances in hand, strolled up the pleasant pathway through the beech-woods to Hammerpond Park, and pitched his apparatus in a strategic position commanding the house. Here he was observed by Mr Raphael Sant, who was returning across the park from a study of the chalk-pits. His curiosity having been fired by Porson's account of the new arrival, he turned aside with the idea of discussing nocturnal art.

Mr Watkins was apparently unaware of his approach. A friendly conversation with Lady Hammerpond's butler had just terminated, and that individual, surrounded by the three pet dogs which it was his duty to take for an airing after dinner had been served, was receding in the distance. Mr Watkins was mixing colour with an air of great industry. Sant, approaching more nearly, was surprised to see the colour in question was as harsh and brilliant an emerald green as it is possible to imagine. Having cultivated an extreme sensibility to colour from his earliest years, he drew the air in sharply between his teeth at the very first glimpse of this brew. Mr Watkins turned round. He looked annoyed.

"What on earth are you going to do with that *beastly* green?" said Sant.

Mr Watkins realised that his zeal to appear busy in the eyes of the butler had evidently betrayed him into some technical error. He looked at Sant and hesitated.

"Pardon my rudeness," said Sant; "but really, that green is altogether too amazing. It came as a shock. What *do* you mean to do with it?"

Mr Watkins was collecting his resources. Nothing could save the situation but decision. "If you come here interrupting my work," he said, "I'm a-goin' to paint your face with it."

Sant retired, for he was a humourist and a peaceful man. Going down the hill he met Porson and Wainwright. "Either that man is a genius or he is a dangerous lunatic," said he. "Just go up and look at his green." And he continued his way, his countenance brightened by a pleasant anticipation of a cheerful affray round an easel in the gloaming, and the shedding of much green paint.

But to Porson and Wainwright Mr Watkins was less aggressive, and explained that the green was intended to be the first coating of his picture. It was, he admitted in response to a remark, an absolutely new method, invented by himself. But subsequently he became more reticent; he explained he was not going to tell every passer-by the secret of his own particular style, and added some scathing remarks upon the meanness of people "hanging about" to pick up such tricks of the masters as they could, which immediately relieved him of their company.

Twilight deepened, first one then another star appeared. The rooks amid the tall trees to the left of the house had long since lapsed into slumbrous silence, the house itself lost all the details of its architecture and became a dark grey outline, and then the windows of the salon shone out brilliantly, the conservatory was lighted up, and here and there a bedroom window burnt yellow. Had anyone approached the easel in the park it would have been found deserted. One brief uncivil word in brilliant green sullied the purity of its canvas. Mr Watkins was busy in the shrubbery with his assistant, who had discreetly joined him from the carriage-drive.

Mr Watkins was inclined to be self-congratulatory upon the ingenious device by which he had carried all his apparatus boldly, and in the sight of all men, right up to the scene of operations. "That's the dressing-room," he said to his assistant, "and, as soon as the maid takes the candle away and goes down to supper, we'll call in. My! how nice the house do look, to be sure, against the starlight, and with all its windows and lights! Swopme, Jim, I almost wish I *was* a painter-chap. Have you fixed that there wire across the path from the laundry?"

He cautiously approached the house until he stood below the dressing-room window, and began to put together his folding ladder. He was much too experienced a practitioner to feel any unusual excitement. Jim was reconnoitring the smoking-room. Suddenly, close beside Mr Watkins in the bushes, there was a violent crash and a stifled curse. Someone had tumbled over the wire which his assistant had just arranged. He heard feet running on the gravel pathway beyond. Mr Watkins, like all true artists, was a singularly shy man, and he incontinently dropped his folding ladder and began running circumspectly through the shrubbery. He was indistinctly aware of two people hot upon his heels, and he fancied that he distinguished the outline of his assistant in front of him. In another moment he had vaulted the low stone wall bounding the shrubbery, and was in the open park. Two thuds on the turf followed his own leap.

It was a close chase in the darkness through the trees. Mr Watkins was a loosely-built man and in good training, and he gained hand-over-hand upon the hoarsely panting figure in front. Neither spoke, but, as Mr Watkins pulled up alongside, a qualm of awful doubt came over him. The other man turned his head at the same moment and gave an exclamation of surprise. "It's not Jim," thought Mr Watkins, and simultaneously the stranger flung himself, as it were, at Watkin's knees, and they were forthwith grappling on the ground together. "Lend a hand, Bill," cried the stranger as the third man came up. And Bill did—two hands in fact, and some accentuated feet. The fourth man, presumably Jim, had apparently turned aside and made off in a different direction. At any rate, he did not join the trio.

Mr Watkins' memory of the incidents of the next two minutes is extremely vague. He has a dim recollection of having his thumb in the corner of the mouth of the first man, and feeling anxious about its safety, and for some seconds at least he held the head of the gentleman answering to the name of Bill, to the ground by the hair. He was also kicked in a great number of different places, apparently by a vast multitude of people. Then the gentleman who was not Bill got his knee below Mr Watkins' diaphragm, and tried to curl him up upon it.

When his sensations became less entangled he was sitting upon the turf, and eight or ten men—the night was dark, and he was rather too confused to count— standing round him, apparently waiting for him to recover. He mournfully assumed that he was captured, and would probably have made some philosophical reflections on the fickleness of fortune, had not his internal sensations disinclined him for speech.

He noticed very quickly that his wrists were not handcuffed, and then a flask of brandy was put in his hands. This touched him a little—it was such unexpected kindness.

"He's a-comin' round," said a voice which he fancied he recognised as belonging to the Hammerpond second footman.

"We've got 'em, sir, both of 'em," said the Hammerpond butler, the man who had handed him the flask. "Thanks to *you*."

No one answered this remark. Yet he failed to see how it applied to him.

"He's fair dazed," said a strange voice; "the villains half-murdered him."

Mr Teddy Watkins decided to remain fair dazed until he had a better grasp of the situation. He perceived that two of the black figures round him stood side-by-side with a dejected air, and there was something in the carriage of their shoulders that suggested to his experienced eye hands that were bound together. Two! In a flash he rose to his position. He emptied the little flask and staggered—obsequious hands assisting him—to his feet. There was a sympathetic murmur.

"Shake hands, sir, shake hands," said one of the figures near him. "Permit me to introduce myself. I am very greatly indebted to you. It was the jewels of my wife, Lady Aveling, which attracted these scoundrels to the house."

"Very glad to make your lordship's acquaintance," said Teddy Watkins.

"I presume you saw the rascals making for the shrubbery, and dropped down on them?"

"That's exactly how it happened," said Mr Watkins.

"You should have waited till they got in at the window," said Lord Aveling; "they would get it hotter if they had actually committed the burglary. And it was lucky for you two of the policemen were out by the gates, and followed up the three of you. I doubt if you could have secured the two of them—though it was confoundedly plucky of you, all the same."

"Yes, I ought to have thought of all that," said Mr Watkins; "but one can't think of everythink."

"Certainly not," said Lord Aveling. "I am afraid they have mauled you a little," he added. The party was now moving towards the house. "You walk rather lame. May I offer you my arm?"

And instead of entering Hammerpond House by the dressing-room window, Mr Watkins entered it—slightly intoxicated, and inclined now to cheerfulness again—on the arm of a real live peer, and by the front door. "This," thought Mr Watkins, "is burgling in style!" The "scoundrels," seen by the gaslight, proved to be mere local amateurs unknown to Mr Watkins, and they were taken down into the pantry and there watched over by the three policemen, two gamekeepers with loaded guns, the butler, an ostler, and a carman, until the dawn allowed of their removal to Hazelhurst police-station. Mr Watkins was made much of in the saloon. They devoted a sofa to him, and would not hear of a return to the village that night. Lady Aveling was sure he was brilliantly original, and said her idea of Turner was just such another rough, half-inebriated, deep-eyed, brave, and clever man. Some one brought up a remarkable little folding-ladder that had been picked up in the shrubbery, and showed him how it was put together. They also described how wires had been found in the shrubbery, evidently placed there to trip-up unwary pursuers. It was lucky he had escaped these snares. And they showed him the jewels.

Mr Watkins had the sense not to talk too much, and in any conversational difficulty fell back on his internal pains. At last he was seized with stiffness in the back, and yawning. Everyone suddenly awoke to the fact that it was a shame to keep him talking after his affray, so he retired early to his room, the little red room next to Lord Aveling's suite.

The dawn found a deserted easel bearing a canvas with a green inscription, in the Hammerpond Park, and it found Hammerpond House in commotion. But if the dawn found Mr Teddy Watkins and the Aveling diamonds, it did not communicate the information to the police.

A MOTH—GENUS NOVO

Probably you have heard of Hapley—not W.T. Hapley, the son, but the celebrated Hapley, the Hapley of *Periplaneta Hapliia*, Hapley the entomologist. If so you know at least of the great feud between Hapley and Professor Pawkins. Though certain of its consequences may be new to you. For those who have not, a word or two of explanation is necessary, which the idle reader may go over with a glancing eye, if his indolence so incline him.

It is amazing how very widely diffused is the ignorance of such really important matters as this Hapley-Pawkins feud. Those epoch-making controversies, again, that have convulsed the Geological Society, are, I verily believe, almost entirely unknown outside the fellowship of that body. I have heard men of fair general education even refer to the great scenes at these meetings as vestry-meeting squabbles. Yet the great Hate of the English and Scotch geologists has lasted now half a century, and has "left deep and abundant marks upon the body of the science." And this Hapley-Pawkins business, though perhaps a more personal affair, stirred passions as profound, if not profounder. Your common man has no conception of the zeal that animates a scientific investigator, the fury of contradiction you can arouse in him. It is the *odium theologicum* in a new form. There are men, for instance, who would gladly burn Professor Ray Lankester at Smithfield for his treatment of the Mollusca in the Encyclopaedia. That fantastic extension of the Cephalopods to cover the Pteropods ... But I wander from Hapley and Pawkins.

It began years and years ago, with a revision of the Microlepidoptera (whatever these may be) by Pawkins, in which he extinguished a new species created by Hapley. Hapley, who was always quarrelsome, replied by a stinging impeachment of the entire classification of Pawkins. [2]Pawkins, in his "Rejoinder," s[3]uggested that Hapley's microscope was as defective as his powers of observation, and called him an "irresponsible meddler"—Hapley was not a professor at that time. Hapley, in his retort, spok[4]e of "blundering collectors," and described, as if inadvertently, Pawkins' revision as a "miracle of ineptitude." It was war to the knife. However, it would scarcely interest the reader to detail how these two great men quarrelled, and how the split between them widened until from the Microlepidoptera they were at war upon every open question in entomology. There were memorable occasions. At times the Royal Entomological Society meetings resembled nothing so much as the Chamber of Deputies. On the whole, I fancy Pawkins was nearer the

[2] "Remarks on a Recent Revision of Microlepidoptera." *Quart. Journ. Entomological Soc.* 1863.

[3] "Rejoinder to certain Remarks," &c. *Ibid.* 1864.

[4] "Further Remarks," &c. *Ibid.*

truth than Hapley. But Hapley was skilful with his rhetoric, had a turn for ridicule rare in a scientific man, was endowed with vast energy, and had a fine sense of injury in the matter of the extinguished species; while Pawkins was a man of dull presence, prosy of speech, in shape not unlike a water-barrel, over-conscientious with testimonials, and suspected of jobbing museum appointments. So the young men gathered round Hapley and applauded him. It was a long struggle, vicious from the beginning, and growing at last to pitiless antagonism. The successive turns of fortune, now an advantage to one side and now to another—now Hapley tormented by some success of Pawkins, and now Pawkins outshone by Hapley, belong rather to the history of entomology than to this story.

But in 1891 Pawkins, whose health had been bad for some time, published some work upon the "mesoblast" of the Death's Head Moth. What the mesoblast of the Death's Head Moth may be, does not matter a rap in this story. But the work was far below his usual standard, and gave Hapley an opening he had coveted for years. He must have worked night and day to make the most of his advantage.

In an elaborate critique he rent Pawkins to tatters—one can fancy the man's disordered black hair, and his queer dark eyes flashing as he went for his antagonist—and Pawkins made a reply, halting, ineffectual, with painful gaps of silence, and yet malignant. There was no mistaking his will to wound Hapley, nor his incapacity to do it. But few of those who heard him—I was absent from that meeting—realised how ill the man was.

Hapley had got his opponent down, and meant to finish him. He followed with a simply brutal attack upon Pawkins, in the form of a paper upon the development of moths in general, a paper showing evidence of a most extraordinary amount of mental labour, and yet couched in a violently controversial tone. Violent as it was, an editorial note witnesses that it was modified. It must have covered Pawkins with shame and confusion of face. It left no loophole; it was murderous in argument, and utterly contemptuous in tone; an awful thing for the declining years of a man's career.

The world of entomologists waited breathlessly for the rejoinder from Pawkins. He would try one, for Pawkins had always been game. But when it came it surprised them. For the rejoinder of Pawkins was to catch the influenza, to proceed to pneumonia, and to die.

It was perhaps as effectual a reply as he could make under the circumstances, and largely turned the current of feeling against Hapley. The very people who had most gleefully cheered on those gladiators became serious at the consequence. There could be no reasonable doubt the fret of the defeat had contributed to the death of Pawkins. There was a limit even to scientific controversy, said serious people. Another crushing attack was already in the press and appeared on the day before the funeral. I don't think Hapley exerted himself to stop it. People remembered how Hapley had hounded down his rival, and forgot that rival's defects. Scathing satire reads ill over fresh mould. The thing provoked comment in the daily papers. This it was that made me think that you had probably heard of Hapley and this controversy. But, as I have already remarked, scientific workers live very much in a world of their own; half the people, I dare say, who go along Piccadilly to the Academy every year, could not tell you where the learned societies abide. Many even think that Research is a kind of happy-family cage in which all kinds of men lie down together in peace.

In his private thoughts Hapley could not forgive Pawkins for dying. In the first place, it was a mean dodge to escape the absolute pulverisation Hapley had in hand for him, and in the second, it left Hapley's mind with a queer gap in it. For twenty years he had worked hard, sometimes far into the night, and seven days a week, with microscope, scalpel, collecting-net, and pen, and almost entirely with reference to Pawkins. The European reputation he had won had come as an incident in that great antipathy. He had gradually worked up to a climax in this last controversy. It had killed Pawkins, but it had also thrown Hapley out of gear, so to speak, and his doctor advised him to give up work for a time, and rest. So Hapley went down into a quiet village in Kent, and thought day and night of Pawkins, and good things it was now impossible to say about him.

At last Hapley began to realise in what direction the pre-occupation tended. He determined to make a fight for it, and started by trying to read novels. But he could not get his mind off Pawkins, white in the face, and making his last speech— every sentence a beautiful opening for Hapley. He turned to fiction—and found it had no grip on him. He read the "Island Nights' Entertainments" until his "sense of causation" was shocked beyond endurance by the Bottle Imp. Then he went to Kipling, and found he "proved nothing," besides being irreverent and vulgar. These scientific people have their limitations. Then unhappily, he tried Besant's "Inner House," and the opening chapter set his mind upon learned societies and Pawkins at once.

So Hapley turned to chess, and found it a little more soothing. He soon mastered the moves and the chief gambits and commoner closing positions, and began to beat the Vicar. But then the cylindrical contours of the opposite king began to resemble Pawkins standing up and gasping ineffectually against Check-mate, and Hapley decided to give up chess.

Perhaps the study of some new branch of science would after all be better diversion. The best rest is change of occupation. Hapley determined to plunge at diatoms, and had one of his smaller microscopes and Halibut's monograph sent down from London. He thought that perhaps if he could get up a vigorous quarrel with Halibut, he might be able to begin life afresh and forget Pawkins. And very soon he was hard at work, in his habitual strenuous fashion, at these microscopic denizens of the way-side pool.

It was on the third day of the diatoms that Hapley became aware of a novel addition to the local fauna. He was working late at the microscope, and the only light in the room was the brilliant little lamp with the special form of green shade. Like all experienced microscopists, he kept both eyes open. It is the only way to avoid excessive fatigue. One eye was over the instrument, and bright and distinct before that was the circular field of the microscope, across which a brown diatom was slowly moving. With the other eye Hapley saw, as it were, without seeing. He was[5] only dimly conscious of the brass side of the instrument, the illuminated part of the table-cloth, a sheet of note-paper, the foot of the lamp, and the darkened room beyond.

Suddenly his attention drifted from one eye to the other. The table-cloth was of the material called tapestry by shopmen, and rather brightly coloured. The pattern was in gold, with a small amount of crimson and pale blue upon a greyish ground. At one point the pattern seemed displaced, and there was a vibrating movement of the colours at this point.

Hapley suddenly moved his head back and looked with both eyes. His mouth fell open with astonishment.

It was a large moth or butterfly; its wings spread in butterfly fashion!

It was strange it should be in the room at all, for the windows were closed. Strange that it should not have attracted his attention when fluttering to its present position. Strange that it should match the table-cloth. Stranger far that to him, Hapley, the great entomologist, it was altogether unknown. There was no delusion. It was crawling slowly towards the foot of the lamp.

"*Genus novo*, by heavens! And in England!" said Hapley, staring.

Then he suddenly thought of Pawkins. Nothing would have maddened Pawkins more…. And Pawkins was dead!

Something about the head and body of the insect became singularly suggestive of Pawkins, just as the chess king had been.

"Confound Pawkins!" said Hapley. "But I must catch this." And, looking round him for some means of capturing the moth, he rose slowly out of his chair. Suddenly the insect rose, struck the edge of the lampshade—Hapley heard the "ping"—and vanished into the shadow.

In a moment Hapley had whipped off the shade, so that the whole room was illuminated. The thing had disappeared, but soon his practised eye detected it upon the wall paper near the door. He went towards it, poising the lamp-shade for capture. Before he was within striking distance, however, it had risen and was fluttering round the room. After the fashion of its kind, it flew with sudden starts and turns, seeming to vanish here and reappear there. Once Hapley struck, and missed; then again.

The third time he hit his microscope. The instrument swayed, struck and over-turned the lamp, and fell noisily upon the floor. The lamp turned over on the table and, very luckily, went out. Hapley was left in the dark. With a start he felt the strange moth blunder into his face.

It was maddening. He had no lights. If he opened the door of the room the thing would get away. In the darkness he saw Pawkins quite distinctly laughing at him. Pawkins had ever an oily laugh. He swore furiously and stamped his foot

---

[5] The reader unaccustomed to microscopes may easily understand this by rolling a newspaper in the form of a tube and looking through it at a book, keeping the other eye open.

on the floor.

There was a timid rapping at the door.

Then it opened, perhaps a foot, and very slowly. The alarmed face of the land-lady appeared behind a pink candle flame; she wore a night-cap over her grey hair and had some purple garment over her shoulders. "What *was* that fearful smash?" she said. "Has anything—" The strange moth appeared fluttering about the chink of the door. "Shut that door!" said Hapley, and suddenly rushed at her.

The door slammed hastily. Hapley was left alone in the dark. Then in the pause he heard his landlady scuttle upstairs, lock her door and drag something heavy across the room and put against it.

It became evident to Hapley that his conduct and appearance had been strange and alarming. Confound the moth! and Pawkins! However, it was a pity to lose the moth now. He felt his way into the hall and found the matches, after sending his hat down upon the floor with a noise like a drum. With the lighted candle he returned to the sitting-room. No moth was to be seen. Yet once for a moment it seemed that the thing was fluttering round his head. Hapley very suddenly decided to give up the moth and go to bed. But he was excited. All night long his sleep was broken by dreams of the moth, Pawkins, and his landlady. Twice in the night he turned out and soused his head in cold water.

One thing was very clear to him. His landlady could not possibly understand about the strange moth, especially as he had failed to catch it. No one but an entomologist would understand quite how he felt. She was probably frightened at his behaviour, and yet he failed to see how he could explain it. He decided to say nothing further about the events of last night. After breakfast he saw her in her garden, and decided to go out to talk to her to reassure her. He talked to her about beans and potatoes, bees, caterpillars, and the price of fruit. She replied in her usual manner, but she looked at him a little suspiciously, and kept walking as he walked, so that there was always a bed of flowers, or a row of beans, or something of the sort, between them. After a while he began to feel singularly irritated at this, and to conceal his vexation went indoors and presently went out for a walk.

The moth, or butterfly, trailing an odd flavour of Pawkins with it, kept coming into that walk, though he did his best to keep his mind off it. Once he saw it quite distinctly, with its wings flattened out, upon the old stone wall that runs along the west edge of the park, but going up to it he found it was only two lumps of grey and yellow lichen. "This," said Hapley, "is the reverse of mimicry. Instead of a butterfly looking like a stone, here is a stone looking like a butterfly!" Once something hovered and fluttered round his head, but by an effort of will he drove that impression out of his mind again.

In the afternoon Hapley called upon the Vicar, and argued with him upon theological questions. They sat in the little arbour covered with briar, and smoked as they wrangled. "Look at that moth!" said Hapley, suddenly, pointing to the edge of the wooden table.

"Where?" said the Vicar.

"You don't see a moth on the edge of the table there?" said Hapley.

"Certainly not," said the Vicar.

Hapley was thunderstruck. He gasped. The Vicar was staring at him. Clearly the man saw nothing. "The eye of faith is no better than the eye of science," said Hapley, awkwardly.

"I don't see your point," said the Vicar, thinking it was part of the argument.

That night Hapley found the moth crawling over his counterpane. He sat on the edge of the bed in his shirt-sleeves and reasoned with himself. Was it pure hallucination? He knew he was slipping, and he battled for his sanity with the same silent energy he had formerly displayed against Pawkins. So persistent is mental habit, that he felt as if it were still a struggle with Pawkins. He was well versed in psychology. He knew that such visual illusions do come as a result of mental strain. But the point was, he did not only *see* the moth, he had heard it when it touched the edge of the lampshade, and afterwards when it hit against the wall, and he had felt it strike his face in the dark.

He looked at it. It was not at all dreamlike, but perfectly clear and solid-looking in the candle-light. He saw the hairy body, and the short feathery antennae, the jointed legs, even a place where the down was rubbed from the wing. He suddenly felt angry with himself for being afraid of a little insect.

His landlady had got the servant to sleep with her that night, because she was afraid to be alone. In addition she had locked the door, and put the chest of drawers against it. They listened and talked in whispers after they had gone to bed, but nothing occurred to alarm them. About eleven they had ventured to put the candle out, and had both dozed off to sleep. They woke up with a start, and sat up in bed, listening in the darkness.

Then they heard slippered feet going to and fro in Hapley's room. A chair was overturned, and there was a violent dab at the wall. Then a china mantel ornament smashed upon the fender. Suddenly the door of the room opened, and they heard him upon the landing. They clung to one another, listening. He seemed to be dancing upon the staircase. Now he would go down three or four steps quickly, then up again, then hurry down into the hall. They heard the umbrella stand go over, and the fanlight break. Then the bolt shot and the chain rattled. He was opening the door.

They hurried to the window. It was a dim grey night; an almost unbroken sheet of watery cloud was sweeping across the moon, and the hedge and trees in front of the house were black against the pale roadway. They saw Hapley, looking like a ghost in his shirt and white trousers, running to and fro in the road, and beating the air. Now he would stop, now he would dart very rapidly at something invisible, now he would move upon it with stealthy strides. At last he went out of sight up the road towards the down. Then, while they argued who should go down and lock the door, he returned. He was walking very fast, and he came straight into the house, closed the door carefully, and went quietly up to his bedroom. Then everything was silent.

"Mrs Colville," said Hapley, calling down the staircase next morning. "I hope I did not alarm you last night."

"You may well ask that!" said Mrs Colville.

"The fact is, I am a sleep-walker, and the last two nights I have been without my sleeping mixture. There is nothing to be alarmed about, really. I am sorry I made such an ass of myself. I will go over the down to Shoreham, and get some stuff to make me sleep soundly. I ought to have done that yesterday."

But half-way over the down, by the chalk pits, the moth came upon Hapley again. He went on, trying to keep his mind upon chess problems, but it was no good. The thing fluttered into his face, and he struck at it with his hat in self-defence. Then rage, the old rage—the rage he had so often felt against Pawkins—came upon him again. He went on, leaping and striking at the eddying insect. Suddenly he trod on nothing, and fell headlong.

There was a gap in his sensations, and Hapley found himself sitting on the heap of flints in front of the opening of the chalkpits, with a leg twisted back under him. The strange moth was still fluttering round his head. He struck at it with his hand, and turning his head saw two men approaching him. One was the village doctor. It occurred to Hapley that this was lucky. Then it came into his mind, with extraordinary vividness, that no one would ever be able to see the strange moth except himself, and that it behoved him to keep silent about it.

Late that night, however, after his broken leg was set, he was feverish and forgot his self-restraint. He was lying flat on his bed, and he began to run his eyes round the room to see if the moth was still about. He tried not to do this, but it was no good. He soon caught sight of the thing resting close to his hand, by the night-light, on the green table-cloth. The wings quivered. With a sudden wave of anger he smote at it with his fist, and the nurse woke up with a shriek. He had missed it.

"That moth!" he said; and then, "It was fancy. Nothing!"

All the time he could see quite clearly the insect going round the cornice and darting across the room, and he could also see that the nurse saw nothing of it and looked at him strangely. He must keep himself in hand. He knew he was a lost man if he did not keep himself in hand. But as the night waned the fever grew upon him, and the very dread he had of seeing the moth made him see it. About five, just as the dawn was grey, he tried to get out of bed and catch it, though his leg was afire with pain. The nurse had to struggle with him.

On account of this, they tied him down to the bed. At this the moth grew bolder, and once he felt it settle in his hair. Then, because he struck out violently with his arms, they tied these also. At this the moth came and crawled over his face, and Hapley wept, swore, screamed, prayed for them to take it off him, unavailingly.

The doctor was a blockhead, a half-qualified general practitioner, and quite ignorant of mental science. He simply said there was no moth. Had he possessed the wit, he might still, perhaps, have saved Hapley from his fate by entering into his delusion and covering his face with gauze, as he prayed might be done. But, as I say, the doctor was a blockhead, and until the leg was healed Hapley was kept tied to his bed, and with the imaginary moth crawling over him. It never left him while he was awake and it grew to a monster in his dreams. While he was awake he longed for sleep, and from sleep he awoke screaming.

So now Hapley is spending the remainder of his days in a padded room, worried by a moth that no one else can see. The asylum doctor calls it hallucination; but Hapley, when he is in his easier mood, and can talk, says it is the ghost of Pawkins, and consequently a unique specimen and well worth the trouble of catching.

THE TREASURE IN THE FOREST

The canoe was now approaching the land. The bay opened out, and a gap in the white surf of the reef marked where the little river ran out to the sea; the thicker and deeper green of the virgin forest showed its course down the distant hill slope. The forest here came close to the beach. Far beyond, dim and almost cloudlike in texture, rose the mountains, like suddenly frozen waves. The sea was still save for an almost imperceptible swell. The sky blazed.

The man with the carved paddle stopped. "It should be somewhere here," he said. He shipped the paddle and held his arms out straight before him.

The other man had been in the fore part of the canoe, closely scrutinising the land. He had a sheet of yellow paper on his knee.

"Come and look at this, Evans," he said.

Both men spoke in low tones, and their lips were hard and dry.

The man called Evans came swaying along the canoe until he could look over his companion's shoulder.

The paper had the appearance of a rough map. By much folding it was creased and worn to the pitch of separation, and the second man held the discoloured fragments together where they had parted. On it one could dimly make out, in almost obliterated pencil, the outline of the bay.

"Here," said Evans, "is the reef and here is the gap." He ran his thumb-nail over the chart.

"This curved and twisting line is the river—I could do with a drink now!—and this star is the place."

"You see this dotted line," said the man with the map; "it is a straight line, and runs from the opening of the reef to a clump of palm-trees. The star comes just where it cuts the river. We must mark the place as we go into the lagoon."

"It's queer," said Evans, after a pause, "what these little marks down here are for. It looks like the plan of a house or something; but what all these little dashes, pointing this way and that, may mean I can't get a notion. And what's the writing?"

"Chinese," said the man with the map.

"Of course! *He* was a Chinee," said Evans.

"They all were," said the man with the map.

They both sat for some minutes staring at the land, while the canoe drifted slowly. Then Evans looked towards the paddle.

"Your turn with the paddle now, Hooker," said he.

And his companion quietly folded up his map, put it in his pocket, passed Evans carefully, and began to paddle. His movements were languid, like those of a man whose strength was nearly exhausted. Evans sat with his eyes half closed, watching the frothy breakwater of the coral creep nearer and nearer. The sky was like a furnace now, for the sun was near the zenith. Though they were so near the Treasure he did not feel the exaltation he had anticipated. The intense excitement of the struggle for the plan, and the long night voyage from the mainland in the unprovisioned canoe had, to use his own expression, "taken it out of him." He tried to arouse himself by directing his mind to the ingots the Chinamen had spoken of, but it would not rest there; it came back headlong to the thought of sweet water rippling in the river, and to the almost unendurable dryness of his lips and throat. The rhythmic wash of the sea upon the reef was becoming audible now, and it had a pleasant sound in his ears; the water washed along the side of the canoe, and the paddle dripped between each stroke. Presently he began to doze.

He was still dimly conscious of the island, but a queer dream texture interwove with his sensations. Once again it was the night when he and Hooker had hit upon the Chinamen's secret; he saw the moonlit trees, the little fire burning, and the black figures of the three Chinamen—silvered on one side by moonlight, and on the other glowing from the firelight—and heard them talking together in pigeon-English—for they came from different provinces. Hooker had caught the drift of their talk first, and had motioned to him to listen. Fragments of the conversation were inaudible and fragments incomprehensible. A Spanish galleon from the Philippines hopelessly aground, and its treasure buried against the day of return, lay in the background of the story; a shipwrecked crew thinned by disease, a quarrel or so, and the needs of discipline, and at last taking to their boats never to be heard of again. Then Chang-hi, only a year since, wandering ashore, had happened upon the ingots hidden for two hundred years, had deserted his junk, and reburied them with infinite toil, single-handed but very safe. He laid great stress on the safety—it was a secret of his. Now he wanted help to return and exhume them. Presently the little map fluttered and the voices sank. A fine story for two stranded British wastrels to hear! Evans' dream shifted to the moment when he had Chang-hi's pigtail in his hand. The life of a Chinaman is scarcely sacred like a European's. The cunning little face of Chang-hi, first keen and furious like a startled snake, and then fearful, treacherous and pitiful, became overwhelmingly prominent in the dream. At the end Chang-hi had grinned, a most incomprehensible and startling grin. Abruptly things became very unpleasant, as they will do at times in dreams. Chang-hi gibbered and threatened him. He saw in his dream heaps and heaps of gold, and Chang-hi intervening and struggling to hold him back from it. He took Chang-hi by the pigtail—how big the yellow brute was, and how he struggled and grinned! He kept growing bigger, too. Then the bright heaps of gold turned to a roaring furnace, and a vast devil, surprisingly like Chang-hi, but with a huge black tail, began to feed him with coals. They burnt his mouth horribly. Another devil was shouting his name: "Evans, Evans, you sleepy fool!" — or was it Hooker?

He woke up. They were in the mouth of the lagoon.

"There are the three palm-trees. It must be in a line with that clump of bushes," said his companion. "Mark that. If we go to those bushes and then strike into the bush in a straight line from here, we shall come to it when we come to the stream."

They could see now where the mouth of the stream opened out. At the sight of it Evans revived. "Hurry up, man," he said, "Or by heaven I shall have to drink sea water!" He gnawed his hand and stared at the gleam of silver among the rocks and green tangle.

Presently he turned almost fiercely upon Hooker. "Give *me* the paddle," he said.

So they reached the river mouth. A little way up Hooker took some water in the hollow of his hand, tasted it, and spat it out. A little further he tried again. "This will do," he said, and they began drinking eagerly.

"Curse this!" said Evans, suddenly. "It's too slow." And, leaning dangerously over the fore part of the canoe, he began to suck up the water with his lips.

Presently they made an end of drinking, and, running the canoe into a little creek, were about to land among the thick growth that overhung the water.

"We shall have to scramble through this to the beach to find our bushes and get the line to the place," said Evans.

"We had better paddle round," said Hooker.

So they pushed out again into the river and paddled back down it to the sea, and along the shore to the place where the clump of bushes grew. Here they landed, pulled the light canoe far up the beach, and then went up towards the edge of the jungle until they could see the opening of the reef and the bushes in a straight line. Evans had taken a native implement out of the canoe. It was L-shaped, and the transverse piece was armed with polished stone. Hooker carried the paddle. "It is straight now in this direction," said he; "we must push through this till we strike the stream. Then we must prospect."

They pushed through a close tangle of reeds, broad fronds, and young trees, and at first it was toilsome going, but very speedily the trees became larger and the ground beneath them opened out. The blaze of the sunlight was replaced by insensible degrees by cool shadow. The trees became at last vast pillars that rose up to a canopy of greenery far overhead. Dim white flowers hung from their stems, and ropy creepers swung from tree to tree. The shadow deepened. On the ground, blotched fungi and a red-brown incrustation became frequent.

Evans shivered. "It seems almost cold here after the blaze outside."

"I hope we are keeping to the straight," said Hooker.

Presently they saw, far ahead, a gap in the sombre darkness where white shafts of hot sunlight smote into the forest. There also was brilliant green undergrowth, and coloured flowers. Then they heard the rush of water.

"Here is the river. We should be close to it now," said Hooker.

The vegetation was thick by the river bank. Great plants, as yet unnamed, grew among the roots of the big trees, and spread rosettes of huge green fans towards the strip of sky. Many flowers and a creeper with shiny foliage clung to the exposed stems. On the water of the broad, quiet pool which the treasure seekers now overlooked there floated big oval leaves and a waxen, pinkish-white flower not unlike a water-lily. Further, as the river bent away from them, the water suddenly frothed and became noisy in a rapid.

"Well?" said Evans.

"We have swerved a little from the straight," said Hooker. "That was to be expected."

He turned and looked into the dim cool shadows of the silent forest behind them. "If we beat a little way up and down the stream we should come to something."

"You said —" began Evans.

"*He* said there was a heap of stones," said Hooker.

The two men looked at each other for a moment.

"Let us try a little down-stream first," said Evans.

They advanced slowly, looking curiously about them. Suddenly Evans stopped. "What the devil's that?" he said.

Hooker followed his finger. "Something blue," he said. It had come into view as they topped a gentle swell of the ground. Then he began to distinguish what it was.

He advanced suddenly with hasty steps, until the body that belonged to the limp hand and arm had become visible. His grip tightened on the implement he carried. The thing was the figure of a Chinaman lying on his face. The *abandon* of the pose was unmistakable.

The two men drew closer together, and stood staring silently at this ominous dead body. It lay in a clear space among the trees. Near by was a spade after the Chinese pattern, and further off lay a scattered heap of stones, close to a freshly dug hole.

"Somebody has been here before," said Hooker, clearing his throat.

Then suddenly Evans began to swear and rave, and stamp upon the ground.

Hooker turned white but said nothing. He advanced towards the prostrate body. He saw the neck was puffed and purple, and the hands and ankles swollen. "Pah!" he said, and suddenly turned away and went towards the excavation. He gave a cry of surprise. He shouted to Evans, who was following him slowly.

"You fool! It's all right It's here still." Then he turned again and looked at the dead Chinaman, and then again at the hole.

Evans hurried to the hole. Already half exposed by the ill-fated wretch beside them lay a number of dull yellow bars. He bent down in the hole, and, clearing off the soil with his bare hands, hastily pulled one of the heavy masses out. As he did so a little thorn pricked his hand. He pulled the delicate spike out with his fingers and lifted the ingot.

"Only gold or lead could weigh like this," he said exultantly.

Hooker was still looking at the dead Chinaman. He was puzzled.

"He stole a march on his friends," he said at last. "He came here alone, and some poisonous snake has killed him … I wonder how he found the place."

Evans stood with the ingot in his hands. What did a dead Chinaman signify? "We shall have to take this stuff to the mainland piecemeal, and bury it there for a while. How shall we get it to the canoe?"

He took his jacket off and spread it on the ground, and flung two or three ingots into it. Presently he found that another little thorn had punctured his skin.

"This is as much as we can carry," said he. Then suddenly, with a queer rush of irritation, "What are you staring at?"

Hooker turned to him. "I can't stand … him." He nodded towards the corpse. "It's so like—"

"Rubbish!" said Evans. "All Chinamen are alike."

Hooker looked into his face. "I'm going to bury *that*, anyhow, before I lend a hand with this stuff."

"Don't be a fool, Hooker," said Evans. "Let that mass of corruption bide."

Hooker hesitated, and then his eye went carefully over the brown soil about them. "It scares me somehow," he said.

"The thing is," said Evans, "what to do with these ingots. Shall we re-bury them over here, or take them across the strait in the canoe?"

Hooker thought. His puzzled gaze wandered among the tall tree-trunks, and up into the remote sunlit greenery overhead. He shivered again as his eye rested upon the blue figure of the Chinaman. He stared searchingly among the grey depths between the trees.

"What's come to you, Hooker?" said Evans. "Have you lost your wits?"

"Let's get the gold out of this place, anyhow," said Hooker.

He took the ends of the collar of the coat in his hands, and Evans took the opposite corners, and they lifted the mass. "Which way?" said Evans. "To the canoe?"

"It's queer," said Evans, when they had advanced only a few steps, "but my arms ache still with that paddling."

"Curse it!" he said. "But they ache! I must rest."

They let the coat down. Evans' face was white, and little drops of sweat stood out upon his forehead. "It's stuffy, somehow, in this forest."

Then with an abrupt transition to unreasonable anger: "What is the good of waiting here all the day? Lend a hand, I say! You have done nothing but moon since we saw the dead Chinaman."

Hooker was looking steadfastly at his companion's face. He helped raise the coat bearing the ingots, and they went forward perhaps a hundred yards in silence. Evans began to breathe heavily. "Can't you speak?" he said.

"What's the matter with you?" said Hooker.

Evans stumbled, and then with a sudden curse flung the coat from him. He stood for a moment staring at Hooker, and then with a groan clutched at his own throat.

"Don't come near me," he said, and went and leant against a tree. Then in a steadier voice, "I'll be better in a minute."

Presently his grip upon the trunk loosened, and he slipped slowly down the stem of the tree until he was a crumpled heap at its foot. His hands were clenched convulsively. His face became distorted with pain. Hooker approached him.

"Don't touch me! Don't touch me!" said Evans in a stifled voice. "Put the gold back on the coat."

"Can't I do anything for you?" said Hooker.

"Put the gold back on the coat."

As Hooker handled the ingots he felt a little prick on the ball of his thumb. He looked at his hand and saw a slender thorn, perhaps two inches in length.

Evans gave an inarticulate cry and rolled over.

Hooker's jaw dropped. He stared at the thorn for a moment with dilated eyes. Then he looked at Evans, who was now crumpled together on the ground, his back bending and straitening spasmodically. Then he looked through the pillars of the trees and net-work of creeper stems, to where in the dim grey shadow the blue-clad body of the Chinaman was still indistinctly visible. He thought of the little dashes in the corner of the plan, and in a moment he understood.

"God help me!" he said. For the thorns were similar to those the Dyaks poison and use in their blowing-tubes. He understood now what Chang-hi's assurance of the safety of his treasure meant. He understood that grin now.

"Evans!" he cried.

But Evans was silent and motionless now, save for a horrible spasmodic twitching of his limbs. A profound silence brooded over the forest.

Then Hooker began to suck furiously at the little pink spot on the ball of his thumb—sucking for dear life. Presently he felt a strange aching pain in his arms and shoulders, and his fingers seemed difficult to bend. Then he knew that sucking was no good.

Abruptly he stopped, and sitting down by the pile of ingots, and resting his chin upon his hands and his elbows upon his knees, stared at the distorted but still stirring body of his companion. Chang-hi's grin came in his mind again. The dull pain spread towards his throat and grew slowly in intensity. Far above him a faint breeze stirred the greenery, and the white petals of some unknown flower came floating down through the gloom.

Lector House believes that a society develops through a two-fold approach of continuous learning and adaptation, which is derived from the study of classic literary works spread across the historic timeline of literature records. Therefore, we aim at reviving, repairing and redeveloping all those inaccessible or damaged but historically as well as culturally important literature across subjects so that the future generations may have an opportunity to study and learn from past works to embark upon a journey of creating a better future.

This book is a result of an effort made by Lector House towards making a contribution to the preservation and repair of original ancient works which might hold historical significance to the approach of continuous learning across subjects.

HAPPY READING & LEARNING!

LECTOR HOUSE LLP
E-MAIL: lectorpublishing@gmail.com